CW00417912

First Printing: 2020 Amazon Publishing
Bristol, UK

www.KimWedlock.com

@KimWedlock


Cover art by Frenone
Used and lightly adjusted
with permission

www.Frenone.net

@Frenone

# Hlífrún

Kim Wedlock

*Thank you so much for your support!*

A particular thank you to
Danni, Kim & James
for beta-reading.

And to Elisa
for her help on translations.

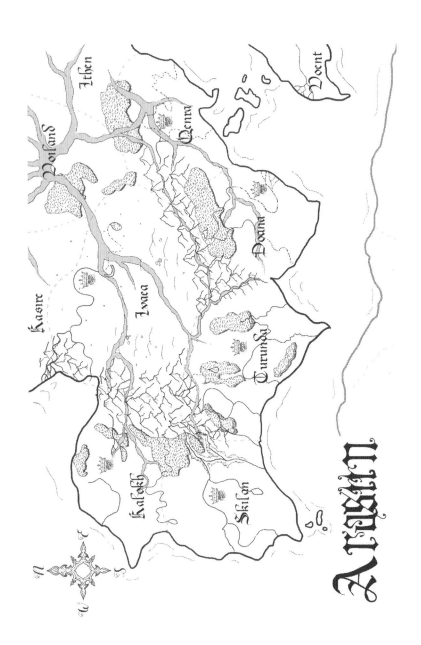

Aragin

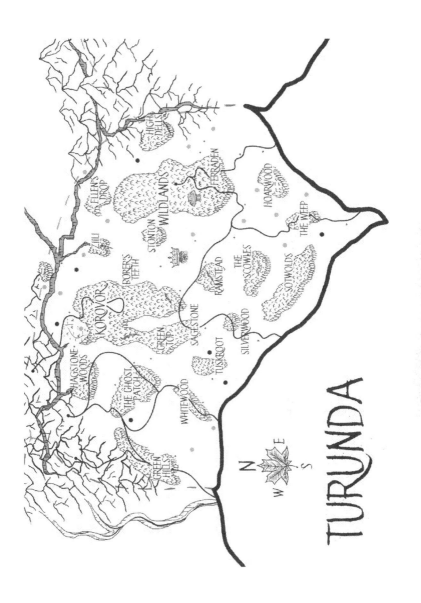

TURUNDA

HIGH FELLS

ELLEN'S DROP

FERNADEN

STONTON WILDLANDS

HOARWOOD

THE WEEP

HILL

BORER'S TEETH

RAKSTEAD

THE SCOWES

COTWOLDS

KOROVOR

GREEN TOP

SAGESTONE

SILVERWOOD

HAGSTONE WOODS

THE GHOST PATCH

TUSKROOT

WHITEWOOD

N

E

S

W

GREEN HILLS

# Prologue

No matter history's lessons, the downfall of civilisation will always repeat itself. It's an eternal failing that stands just a step back in the shadow of success. And it never diminishes; it waits, it broods, and when it takes that single step forwards as Success finally teeters in exhaustion, it strikes with a fury to match its patience. But, as eternal as Doom's presence, its diversity is boundless. Success always takes the same, blatant shape, but Doom is an artist. It is nuanced, it shifts; it never strikes in the same way, and it is never seen coming.

But it is always summoned by the same, foolish circumstances: the powers of civilised peoples.

Terrible in what these powers could achieve, and yet existing purely for their betterment, nothing and no one was safe from them. Even the land fell victim to civilisation's arrogance, razed, flattened and shredded for use. There was no room, when ideas of supremacy or honour arose, for what was good, right or should be, only the need to move forwards and prove themselves strongest. When the improvement of one life diminished another; when the safety of one people endangered another; when the survival of one world destroyed another, and nothing was wrong with either to begin with.

By any means, by any cost, one must always win, and one must always lose. Balance was a thing forgotten.

Turunda, within the war-ravaged continent of Arasiin, was trapped in the most recent recurrence of inevitability and staring directly into the face of Doom. Riven by the unnatural powers of its denizens, the land was suffering, and while its short-sighted men warred, only a few seemed aware of the extent. And among the shackles of civilised expectations, fewer still dared to discomfort themselves and do anything about it.

But though a paltry few were wise enough to chase the root of the problem, the symptoms continued to spiral, and Turunda would surely be dead before they succeeded.

# Chapter 1

A gentle, viridian breath rustled through the world. Weighted by the rich scent of loam and moss, the air pirouetted under the cool tug of the breeze, while the fresh edge of rain cast a welcome division in the long-unbroken midsummer heat. There was promise in that, of life and abundance, and enthusiasm hung like a restless fog stirred up by every other breath.

The air was not silent. The air was *never* silent. Here, there was always some sound of comfort or company, overlapping and interlocking with another into an unrecitable harmony. It was a melody without rhythm, composed of the rustle of dark, summer-kissed leaves, the warble, chirp and trill of birds, the squeak, croak and howl of beasts and the babble of rolling streams. It was a symphony filled with secrets, while the voices of the trees themselves whispered 'welcome, Queen,' into the winds.

She opened her dark eyes and watched the colours of eternal twilight shift through the forest around her, glittering in the fidget of leaves aglow with the sparse leak of sunlight. A pair of woodlarks looped and flitted briefly into view in a dazzling display of iridescent gold, and a beetle tumbled from a tree, landing with a soft thud on the damp moss below.

Then all fell still once again.

Hlífrún's grey lips curved into an insuppressible smile.

Here was serenity. This was a place of ancient souls; a place where time slowed and wandered, the smallest measure that of the passing sun, the longest that of the turning seasons. There was nothing to rush for here, no urgency, no fret. There was only life. All was as it had always been.

...Almost.

Her gaze dropped back to the ground. Her heart sullenly followed as she locked onto the tidy mat of winding roots that stretched forwards for some feet, young, bare and smooth; ash and rowan woven together in a mutual charge to bridge the abyss that rent the otherwise pristine forest.

Though she begged them not to, her eyes followed the line of that gaping wound yet again, searching despite the hole in her heart for a clue of the scale of destruction. Mercifully, the trees spared her that torment. She could already feel the rend all too deeply, as though her own body had been torn. And she supposed it had been, in a way. The spirit of this and every forest was equally her own.

The leaves above fluttered with the heavy shudder of her heart. She drew herself back in with a sigh.

She knelt gracefully in the damp soil, rain water swelling around her knees and trickling through the grooves of her grey, bark-like skin, and slipped a rough, slender hand down through the dirt. The earth bowed aside willingly.

As she closed her eyes and released a slow, focused breath, a fine, off-white sheath began to form around the exposed roots. It crept out across them slowly, spreading like a tangled, fibrous web, sealing where they overlapped and wove together, where they knotted, where they released. Then a second mass responded on the far side of the rift, bleeding through the sheared soil. But it was slower. Sluggish, as though the last drops of its life force were ebbing away, sacrificed for this final growth.

The approaching web ambled closer, creeping further and faster along the roots as though it recognised its kind, and when it burrowed at last into the severed soil, seized and anchored by the woody spears, the second, struggling mass bloomed.

In that instant, the forest changed.

All around, the pockets of grass and wildflowers that had found sun enough to grow stood taller and brighter, their scents intensified, and the branches of the surrounding trees reached higher toward the morning sun. Bark darkened around their trunks, roots thickened and flexed, and the soil that nourished them all swelled and sweetened with vitality.

Pride flared through Hlífrún's blood. She drank in the rejoice of the forest, the tinkling songs of the flowers, the young, twitching voices of grasses, and the rumbling creaks of the ancient trees as each declared their gratitude. Even the air seemed to lift and hum.

The change was glorious.

Her eyes flicked towards another patch of rustling, quivering grass and watched a mole poke its head out from the soil. She beamed gleefully as it squinted towards her, and returned its relieved snuffle with a wriggle of her own nose before it bumbled lazily back into the earth.

This rift was the last of them, at least for the moment. The mykodendrit had been repaired at the most vital locations - its fungal network would heal, and her influence across the continent's forests would repair with it. She could already feel her primordial link to the Vaen Steppes strengthening far in the north.

She stayed there for a while, relishing the summer breeze as it teased her thick, dark mane through her twiggy crown, and bathed in the sounds of her queendom.

Until another concern edged its way to the front of her mind.

She didn't muddy the air with her sigh. She rose instead, lifted her chin, and walked on through the forest to address it.

Midsummer's Day was almost upon them. It was an important day, a crucial one for life, the most vibrant of the year - but it was also a day that was in sore need of vigilance. Humans always built their fires in a preposterous celebration of the sun, and every single one of them seemed to think that they could control the most destructive force of nature. In her thousands of years, she'd never once seen a shred of evidence that suggested they were learning from their mistakes, even as whole villages burned down from a single stray flicker, never mind the forests.

But, the wilds were not helpless to them, especially not with her at their lead. She and its denizens had developed a steady system over the centuries, and while a number of parties needed reminding of their role at almost every such occasion, it remained fairly reliable.

*Fairly.* Unfortunately, humans couldn't always be so easily predicted.

A tangle of juniper parted on her approach, and she stepped through with a distracted thanks.

Her woody fingers were already curling into fists as the most recent of human offences blazed its way to the front of her mind: the blackened, skeletal trees, reaching from the scorched earth like gnarled claws pleading for help; the dead silence that weighted the stifling air more heavily than the heat itself; the woven willow faces of kvistdjur, her loyal forest wardens, charred and crumbling where they lay, unrecognisable, dead, dry and bare of leaves.

She caught herself and loosened her fists, ignoring the sap that oozed from the fresh wounds on her palms.

That day was almost half a century behind her, but the responsibility, the *failure*, remained as if it had been yesterday. She'd fought even harder since to ensure it didn't happen again, but the fear that humans would inevitably find some other way to blindly destroy her domain seemed to dig its roots even deeper into her heart with every passing year.

And so, that morning, her preparations began anew, first with a few polite visits to reinforce the weakest links in her chain of defence - and the näcken and the Arkhamas were perhaps the least reliable of all.

In fairness, the näcken weren't *deliberately* difficult - they didn't fall under her rule, so they couldn't be expected to hear her call to arms through the roots. But her sister, the Mother of Currents, didn't deal as directly with the creatures of her domain as Hlífrún did, and for that reason, the Mother of Roots wasn't above bypassing her and eliciting the river sprites' help herself. They would provide it readily enough - as long as they stood to gain, too. Which, of course, they did: by redirecting the flow of their rivers to put out stray fires or stop them from spreading in the first place, their water would pick up fresh nutrients, and that would benefit *everyone*.

No, the *näcken* were not deliberately difficult.

The Arkhamas, however, *were*.

The short, almost child-like creatures were numerous, loud and impulsive, and seemed to refuse all authority. But their unique ability to communicate silently across vast distances was just as crucial to damage control as the näcken's rivers. And besides, she'd long since found a clever little way to deal with the unruly things.

Hlífrún, stepped from the damp soil and into a birch tree, melding into the bark as though it wasn't there at all.

When she stepped back out, the birch and surrounding forest had become an alderwood, the nearby sound of birdsong had been replaced by cackles, whoops and the sound of clambering feet, and what peace had draped the trees was now an indignant protest. But, whatever the Arkhamas were doing, it was only a minor offence. The older trees got, the more easily offended they became.

She brushed her hand soothingly over the bark as she stepped down to the root-laced soil, and felt their collective disgruntlement fade. Then she started straight towards the racket.

They soon fell into sight: seven of them, their pale skin smeared deliberately with mud, clad in either animal hides or human clothes stolen from washing lines, playing, eating, whittling while one was chasing a weasel. It was a harmless game - if the weasel didn't want to play, it would've been quick to let them know.

It took some time for them to notice her - she'd stepped fully into their glade, in fact, before the weasel felt her presence, and even once it had scurried away from its would-be captor and up onto the tree beside her to nuzzle at her cheek, the rest of them still took a few moments longer to work out why. The trees were looming disapprovingly by that point.

"Yer Majesty!" The weasel-chaser cried, grinning as he finally dashed forwards to greet her. The rest remained stubbornly where they were, on rocks, in the branches, and an eighth poked her head out of a hollow tree trunk. "'Appy Midsummer-Or-There-Abouts! What'n can we do for ya?"

"Happy Midsummer," she smiled despite herself, stroking the weasel's head. As bold and troublesome as Arkhamas were, she couldn't help her affection. Their presence alone always lightened her mood.

A single root rose from the ground and twisted itself into a stool, which she sat upon gratefully, her cow-like tail swaying happily behind her. "It's exactly that which I've come to talk to you about."

Every one of them narrowed their oversized eyes with shared suspicion. A few wandered over her naked body. She smiled sweetly and ignored it. "I have a job for you all."

"*Again?*" One of them groaned.

"Yep, and it's *very* important."

The first boy, one with sticks and bones tied into his matted hair, folded his arms and looked down his snubby nose at her. He had to tilt his head a fair way back to do it. "You said that *last* year."

"And this year," she smiled brightly, "it's even *more* important. The humans will be lighting their Midsummer fires in a matter of days--"

"Why do they do that?"

"Now of all nows, an' all!"

"Yer, it's hot enough, ain't it?"

"--And I need you all to keep your big and wonderful eyes open," she continued over the gaggle.

The bone-haired boy watched her for a moment. They all did,

each sharing their thoughts in silence. Then came the whistle of air being sucked in through chipped teeth. "Sounds like a big respons'bility, Yer Majesty. What with the magic an' all - I mean, there's already a lot we gotta watch out for, ya know..."

"I certainly do," she beamed, "which is why it's such a *very* big responsibility, and why I need your help so *very* much this year. I need you to keep watch for bonfires stacked too close to forests and move them away, I need you to stop anyone from lighting anything too close, and I need you to raise the alarm if anyone *does*."

"Like I said," the boy smiled not quite as sweetly, "*big* responsibility, and a fat lotta work, to boot. Per'aps we'd *all* be better off if'n you just asked your vakeys to do it."

The other Arkhamas began nodding and agreeing - audibly.

She rested her chin in her barkish hand and pretended to ponder the suggestion for a while. Her dark eyebrows drew slowly together. Then her round lips pursed in doubt. "I'm not so sure the vakehn are *capable* of this kind of job. I mean, it takes a certain kind of strength and determination to face humans, wouldn't you say? I mean, if they *could* do it, I would've asked them already. After all, I know how dreadfully busy you all are..."

Their eyes narrowed again.

"No," she sighed, "I'm afraid only *Arkhamas* can do it."

The bone-haired boy grunted. "Well, that's a shame then, ain't it? 'Cause we're just tooooo busy. Like you said yerself, 'Majesty."

She sighed and rose to her feet. A flicker of victory passed over the Arkhamas's faces until they noticed that she, too, was smiling. "Thank you," she beamed.

The forest children blinked at her as the root stool unravelled and returned to the ground. "What?"

"I appreciate your help, Gaz," she sang, turning her tree-hollow back towards them and stepping away into the trees. "I really don't know *what* I'd do without you!"

"H-hey, wait, what--"

"You'd better spread the word right away and move out to the borders, or you might miss something!"

"Bu-bu-but," Gaz reached out after her as the others scrambled to their feet in confusion, "we didn't agree to *nothin'!*"

"Thank you, my dearests! I appreciate your co-operation, so *very* much!" Then she stepped into a tree and vanished - though she remained in there just long enough to hear the defeated groan waft out through the glade.

When she stepped out again, the alderwoods had shifted to willows leaning silently along a river bank. She wended and wove her way among them, following the deep, flowing river below very carefully, stifling her trepidation. Water was a wonderful, life-giving thing, but unlike the earth, it was somewhat...insubstantial. It had a surface, technically, but there was no physical way to stand on it, and while it was true that her wild magic allowed her the ability to do just that, it still sent a chill through her bones. She *greatly* preferred solid ground - but she wouldn't find a näck that way.

She continued to step carefully, and a musical sound of softly-bowed strings soon rose from further along the river. She smiled and moved a little faster towards it. The beautiful, alluring sound grew louder and sweeter, calling her closer and closer.

Fortunately, she was immune to its magic.

She stopped before the source of the melody and leaned forwards over the water, hanging on to the tree. It lowered her closer on her request.

"You won't lure me in there, I'm afraid," she told her reflection, and waited as the music rose a little louder. She simply smiled and shook her head.

Soon, another face half-rose from the water surface, breaking her reflection - that of a boy much like an Arkhamas, but with green, scaled skin, yellow eyes with the slitted pupils of a frog and long, algae-frond hair that drifted with the flow of the river. Those eyes looked back at her with some degree of irritation. She met them with an unbroken smile. "Now, young man: I need your help."

# Chapter 2

A few days passed; no more rifts had opened in the earth, and the efforts to ward the forests were progressing smoothly. Even the Arkhamas were doing their part - in fact, they'd been the first to begin. So Hlífrún allowed herself a moment of calm before the time came for those defences to be put to the test - assuming they were needed this year.

She lounged in the arms of an ancient chestnut tree and tracked the crooked line of the branch her head rested upon, following it upwards as it split into two, then each of those into three, and higher still along the bough's gnarled, tapering lengths until the thinnest twigs curved and craned their leaves up towards the bright, golden sky.

A warm breeze jostled the drops of the morning's rain from the leaves. She barely flinched as the tiny pocket of downpour freckled her sprawling body, and continued to stare impassively up through the reaches, watching the vague wisps of cloud beyond form, thin and scatter.

Hlífrún soon found her eyes closing, and she relaxed deeper into the tree's cradle, breathing slow and deep as the day rolled by.

Until the sound of feather-light footsteps approached through the damp soil.

She sighed wistfully, but didn't open her eyes. The vakehn weren't as quiet as they thought they were. Humans wouldn't hear them, of course, but she always did - a fact that seemed to unsettle them when she reacted before they could greet her.

Today, however, she let them believe she hadn't noticed and remained at peace in the boughs. Maybe they were just passing by.

"Rötternas Moder."

Her lips formed a hard line at her title. *'Nope, not passing by at all.'*

With another thin sigh, Hlífrún finally sat up in the branches and mustered a smile for the woman below. She couldn't help the immediate sag of her shoulders.

Even on this wonderful day, the young woman hid her smooth,

chestnut skin beneath her claddings - the small, thin garment of lichen, moss and spider silk that served both to break up her lithe form and maintain her modesty.

Her kind were not born of the woods, it had merely adopted them, but despite making a centuries-old place for themselves within it, they'd been unable to shed the need for clothing. It was a remnant of their past lives that most vakehn seemed peculiarly attached to - but this one did, at least, leave bare the pleasant garden of forklet moss that draped her shoulder, and the mazegill mushrooms that clung to her hip.

Hlífrún said nothing about it, though, even as another warm breath of air caressed her own bare skin. "Good morning, Birk," she smiled again, and the vakah bowed her head in return.

"Good morning." She spoke softly, despite her jagged accent. "I apologise for the interruption, but we've been unable to find another stendjur to watch over the last rift. It seems they're all already assigned to others."

Hlífrún sighed and hung her head even as her eyes dragged eastwards. She couldn't see the chasm she'd repaired those few days ago, not from that distance, but she could still feel precisely where it was. "Shame... It shouldn't be a problem, humans don't usually venture this far into these woods, but..." She sighed again. "We can't risk leaving it open to meddling. The trees themselves will have to protect it instead."

She dropped gracefully from the branches and landed lightly upon the soil, smiling as the water swelled up over her toes, then started onwards through the forest, her tail swaying happily behind her.

The vakah's own enjoyment of the sensation didn't show for a moment as she fell in step beside her. "You're still unconcerned?"

"Despite the sight of it," the queen replied, brushing her toes over a tuft of grass as she passed it. "The chasms are a simple matter, as they come. It's magic that remains the issue."

"You've heard nothing else of the Mage?"

She shook her head. "Nothing worthwhile. Since leaving the Wildlands, he's addressed White Barrows in the eastern mountains, but that's all. He left the Eswolds two days ago."

"And you're sure he remains our only hope?"

"Of closing the rifts, no. But of removing the arcane taint

responsible, once for all, yes. But his nemesis now holds his focus. The 'root of the issue', he claims."

"And what will we do in the mean time?" The vakah shrank beneath the power of the queen's red-flecked, painite eyes as she turned her a suddenly scathing gaze.

"We continue," she said, just beneath a hiss, "just as we have been. We will *not* be beaten by so young a race."

Hlífrún caught the wideness of the woman's eyes. She forced herself to calm and flashed a sudden smile of apology. "We can handle this. And we'll handle Midsummer at the same time. Have faith in me, dear Birk."

The vakah straightened, resolution gripping her apple-green eyes. "I have *absolute* faith in you, Rötternas Moder. Feira chose you to reign over the wilds of this land when She created the trees' roots, and you've served the goddess perfectly. But this magic--"

"Is out of my control. This is true - but it will be dealt with." Her flashing gaze trailed off absently into the forest. Her voice followed it. "You saw his eyes," she murmured. "The Mage. He'll see it through. Whatever his mind might tell him, his heart shouts louder. He's just going to do it the way *he* sees fit. Try as I might, I was unable to sway him..." She bit her lip in thought. "He is...strong..."

Though she felt the weight of Birk's stare, she didn't stir from her reminiscence in a hurry.

"For now," she continued eventually, "we keep humans away; protect the infected areas from any who might try to meddle. Then we can keep these chasms contained and my network whole."

The vakah's berry-red lips twisted to form another question, but the words never made it out. A mournful song floated in from some nearby grove in the tangled forest instead.

The grey queen's eyes shifted to molten stone.

Without a word, she parted from the vakah and stormed purposefully towards the tormented dirge. Her lips formed a hard line, knuckles paled as her fists clenched at her sides. The forest seemed to bow back as she passed.

This, too, was the fault of magic; the kvistdjur, the forests' most ancient guardians, were being driven to madness, singing the trees to autumnal sleep at the very height of midsummer when they should *both* have been soaking in the heat and life of the sun. The land wasn't the only thing to suffer for the pursuits of 'civilisation' -

the creatures so intrinsically entwined with it faced the same sickness. *Her* creatures. And she didn't have the antidote. She could only offer them her own wild magic, but nothing she could do with it could fix *this*...

Her tail flicked again as her lips pulled into a snarl. A weasel bounced along merrily beside her for a while, but slunk away in defeat when it failed to elicit a smile.

Magic. *Magic*. A wonderful and terrible force, even when wielded with understanding. But when it was wielded *without*...

The matter was more severe than just a few holes. Holes, she could patch. But these rends, she had to bridge, and that meant choosing pockets of forest to sacrifice so that links could be maintained farther afield. The discarded magic that gathered from careless whims had already shattered the entire northern border, tearing open great rifts as wide as five birch trees were tall, and she'd almost completely lost her connection to the distant northern realms of Hin'ua and Doakhul.

But the magic was drawn sorest to the most ancient places of the continent, which it infected zealously, plaguing them with unnatural lights, weather and music - *changing* things. It tarnished creatures with false faces and skins, cast shattered images of the sun on the underside of leaves, even disjointed the air itself. Other creatures within range of the magic's taint had begun to succumb in other ways, like the kvistdjur in rot and madness.

Her woodlands, her *charge*, were torn - those the humans hadn't burned or flooded - and great wounds had been ripped open in the web of mykodendrit, the fungus that encased the roots of all things, connecting them, communicating between them; the living, breathing network beneath the soil that every individual blade of grass needed in order to survive, be it at the southern edge of Turunda, or the northern reaches of Bashqett.

But *human* homes were not so sorely affected - no, of *course* they weren't - and those that were they simply abandoned and replaced. That was the human way. There was no fixing, only replacing. But a tree could no sooner abandon its home than the blades of grass could beneath it. One and all were left to face the consequences of the guilty's careless actions.

Her heart beat faster as the song burrowed deeper into her skin like a woodworm, and her feet moved quicker through the undergrowth.

'The Emerald Kingdom' - she snarled at the pet name the humans so affectionately gave fair, forested Turunda even as they destroyed it. The country that had long stood as but one small pocket of her own reach, and yet also the bearer of her throne, her seat of power, her heart and soul. And they thought *they* owned it, just as they felt they owned everything else. And they destroyed it. Just as they destroyed everything else.

But she would come out on top in the end. Nature always prevailed. It had to. She wouldn't accept anything less.

The twilight of the forest diminished abruptly before the rose-gold glow of sunlight, soft beams reaching through the downy birch and glittering back from the surface of the rain-swollen mire.

Something splooshed from the slippery rocks as she stormed into the clearing - a frog, or so it wished to be seen - but she gave neither the scene nor the innocuous being a moment of thought.

She splashed through the water, stirring up the scent of algae and damp wood behind her, and when its weight slowed her down, she took to the fallen log-bridge. Thick, round and dampened with a smattering of moss, it would've been a slippery joy to run across had it been any other moment. Now, though, it was far from worth breaking a smile for.

On the far side, a stunted vortex whipped about a single spot on the sodden ground, dragging leaves and droplets into its rotation. And there, at its centre, wailing its haunting lament, floated the kvistdjur's cadaverous, twig-woven form.

Foxfire glowed a healthy green from between ribs of winding and rotting branches. Wooden arms reached out with hands of splinter-sharp talons as if to envelop the entire fen, and the horned and woven bear-skull head hung back in the ardour of her song. Her voice, seeping between the knots and hollows in her chest, rose to a crescendo.

As the leaves of dozens of trees began to fade from summer green to a sickly yellow, grey arms wrapped about the wooden form and held it so very close.

Slowly, the aching lullaby diminished.

The vortex faded, and the kvistdjur stood passive within the embrace of her queen.

The mire fell silent.

In that moment, as the wood creaked and she felt the beat of the foxfire heart thump in time with her own, the queen took a long, ragged breath. Her eyes closed, and she inhaled the scent of wood and spores, trailing her finger over the rotten hollow of a tangled arm. She held the kvistdjur a little tighter. It was a comfort she realised she equally needed.

She knew her fury stemmed truly from impatience. The matter *would* be dealt with, of this she was certain - but just how long would it take? Humans were so...*particular.* They had odd notions about doing things 'the right way', which apparently meant taking their time when there wasn't a moment to lose, and racing off to kill and destroy at the slightest provocation when there was nothing to fire urgency at all.

She loathed that the end of the matter was so far out of her hands.

But...even if this magic, this destruction, *was* the consequence of human greed and their careless need to obtain 'greatness', whatever that meant, she'd resolved long ago that she wouldn't let the forests fall to it, just as they wouldn't fall to Midsummer accidents. Her magic may be different, but it was strong in its own right. With it she ensured the forests and grasslands of the continent flourished, along with every creature that called them home. She wouldn't allow those efforts to fail. She was too old for that - inconceivably.

She was Hlífrún - Rötternas Moder in the old forest tongue, Queen of the Woods, Spirit of the Wilds. She was a skogsrå in form and a guardian in purpose.

Many humans had already forgotten her name - they thought her and her kin now myths. 'Wildlings' as humans referred to them in their tales - the creatures that lived in the woods and ate or enslaved whoever strayed inside. Something to scare children with, something to keep them out of trouble. Something even for the adults to fear, otherwise they'd have been forgotten entirely rather than relegated to fables and legends. Only those who dared despite those grim stories to venture into her forests knew otherwise - but, of course, no one ever believed them.

But that was fine. While it was a shame those fearful fables couldn't be put to use stopping the lighting of bonfires, it *did* keep her domain a little safer in the long-run. Humans so often attacked what they didn't understand; if it had no use or didn't fit into their ideals, it shouldn't exist at all. And so the fewer that ventured into her forests, the better. And those that did usually paid their respects, be it through habit or superstition.

She held the kvistdjur tightly while her shoulders and hollowed back straightened with conviction.

Yes, nature would come out on top in the end. Nature always prevailed.

It had to. Or there would be nothing left.

*Five days.*


*Foreboding laced the air like a poison. There was no shriek or song of bird, there was no buzz or chirp of insect. Even the breeze itself had choked. There was only the faintest hum, an incorporeal tremor, as though something ancient and awful was rumbling awake.*

*Rabbit and raghorn froze and strained against the deafening silence. Eagle and dragonfly observed like stone from their perches. Vittra gathered and muttered apprehensions, kvistdjur stared through the shadows, Arkhamas climbed higher and peered through the branches, näcken watched from beneath crystalline water.*

*Slowly, a glowing white fog took form in the distance. Every eye watched it, fixated with stifled breath as it grew gradually brighter, gradually denser, until it shifted from a mist to a thick, shimmering wall of cloud. They watched as it rolled, engulfing more and more of the forests with every passing second, all while heading inexorably closer.*

*A vague and terrible understanding swept out ahead of it.*

*Instinct scattered them in a heartbeat, flying, burrowing, running and diving, even while their bones promised them it couldn't be escaped.*

*The glittering cloud surged in like a tidal wave.*

# Chapter 3

Flowering meadows and valleys bleached. Lakes and rivers turned to glass. Rain froze mid-fall. Breeze stood still and shimmered with diamonds, the air itself seized by the frigid grasp of magic.

Hlífrún staggered at the trauma a thousand times over. She felt the eastern border rip open as keenly as an axe through her chest, and the cloud of frosted magic ravage the country like a sandstorm, both as unstoppable as the sunset. And when that cloud surged into her view, she hadn't a moment to collect herself before it barrelled right through her, forcing her back a step and peeling away her bark as though it had physically clawed her.

Cold seized in, tightening her chest, but still she stared in horror as a thin sheet of ice glazed the thicket leaf by leaf. It didn't flinch despite the venom in her flaming, incredulous eyes.

In a single moment, her heart broke and stitched back together, and her blood compressed into a boundless rage.

All around her had been leached of motion and colour; her world, her queendom, was muffled into a deathly silence. The birds and squirrels she'd watched frolic fell abruptly still in shock, fur and feathers crystallising as they fought for tiny breaths. Near and far, feet and hooves stamped over rigid grass in torment. Many of the oldest and youngest quickly collapsed in defeat.

Hlífrún spun frantically, stirring the freezing air into a cloud of glassy shards, searching for the cause, for answers, for anything that might halt the ebbing of life that mounted in all corners of her domain and threatened to collapse upon her. For the first time in millennia, she felt fear.

A chorus of sepulchral voices rose up at once from all across the forest, shattering the frozen silence. They tormented her for only a moment before she found her paralysis funnelling rapidly into her fury.

Helplessness was an indulgence she couldn't afford.

Her teeth clenched, steadying her rage into something controllable, and she rushed backwards into the nearest tree, melting into the frosted bark and vanishing from the thicket. When she stepped out of another a moment later, she fought back a lurch of nausea at the sight of her moss, stone and woven root throne splintered and feathered with rime.

Her eyes closed and she pulled her spirit in just as tightly. She had no time for that, either. With effort, she squeezed herself into the centre of her consciousness in this sacred place, took a deep, shaking breath, and scoured for a solution.

Then five pairs of chestnut feet rushed into the yew-shaded glade.

Her lip curled at the interruption, but she managed, somehow, to bite her tongue. The vakehn were not to blame for this - not personally. And, attuned as they were to the natural leys, to what was good and right and real in the world - the things that could *truly* stop the world from turning - they could presently be of use to her. Six minds were better than one.

"Magic," Birk said needlessly, casting that idea into doubt.

"Yes," Hlífrún snarled. "Humans. *Again.*" She snapped back to her throne and hissed at it. "What could they have possibly done?!"

"It's a mistake," another spoke up grimly, "almost certainly."

"Of *course* it is! They haven't got a *clue* how to handle their power! And now," her eyes, sharp as thorns, drank in the tainted forest, "now *we* are in danger. We're not ready for winter. It's too soon, *much* too soon..."

They didn't flinch when she suddenly whirled away, her mane a storm about her shoulders, and thundered from her royal glade. She melted through the briar tangles that couldn't move out of her way fast enough.

The vakehn followed dutifully, fury staining their own eyes as they ran and hopped on two legs as efficiently as deer through the undergrowth.

She stopped at the first patch of light to penetrate the trees and scurried up the trunk of an ancient ash. The askafroa that called it home hissed and shuffled indignantly out along the branches. Hlífrún tried to cast the frightened, twiggy little girl a comforting smile as she passed, but her lips failed to move.

Once again, as she broke through the crown, shock forced the breath from her lungs in a white, swirling mist.

It was not just the ground.

Louring above the carpet of lucent trees, the clouds that had concealed the sun all morning had turned a bloated black-purple, swollen now with snow or hail and the broken promise of rain. They hung as heavy and immovable as a blanket of stone. A blanket that would inevitably come crashing down.

Her woody fingers tightened about the hoar-frosted branches as her body shook in outrage. Midsummer couldn't save them if it couldn't *reach* them; there would be no warm winds to thaw the ice, no rains to slacken its grip. Even the old threats of Midsummer bonfires would've been almost welcome.

There was no knowing how high the magic had reached, and her own - wild, green and pure - couldn't be turned against it. It was incompatible.

This could last for hours or days.

*'No,'* she hissed to herself. *'This is human magic. It will be weeks...'*

An oath the sound of snapping branches cracked from her throat. This time, the askafroa kept her protests to herself.

The Queen of the Woods dropped back to the ground in a billow of ice crystals. The vakehn straightened grimly as she cast dour eyes across them, and spoke in a voice that could've commanded the stars to give up their shine. No one questioned what she'd seen.

"Prepare the forest. Assume the worst. We survived a premature winter when Mount Tolendra erupted two thousand years ago; we can survive this one." Her gaze flicked past them, and she marched back to her ruined glade, vakehn in tow. "Those most delicate must be put to sleep. The kvistdjur must be restrained no longer, infected or not. Their lullabies must be heard, or we'll lose swathes." She stamped her bare foot almost absently through a brook, shattering the solid ice. "And water must flow freely."

"The näcken are troublesome," one of her entourage reminded her, to which she merely shook her twig-crowned head.

"They will listen. They can be trusted to keep their home waters from freezing, they need only extend those efforts. The animals will also need help. And the askafroa - and in aiding them, their trees will remain safe."

"We can handle their care," another vakah assured her, a male, though it could only be seen by the shape of his jaw and the absence of any chest cladding. "And that of the others."

"You'll have to. But...not all of you..." She didn't glance around at their quizzical looks. "I can't reverse this magic. But we can keep the forests alive. The thickest can be warmed, and *not* by fire."

More vakehn had gathered when they emerged back into the glade, and their reverent attention fell upon her in a heartbeat. She looked across them all, one at a time. Their dark skin seemed darker still against the deathly contrast of white, and their shapes were broken up perfectly by their lichen-speckled garments. If not for the heat of their life force, she could've missed them.

Despite searching for suggestions in their eyes, she found herself dubious when one finally stepped forwards with a wary edge to his own. "I apologise, Rötternas Moder, but...you could reach out to *him*..."

None were surprised by the inferno that sparked to life in her piercing painite gaze. He, least of all.

"You expect a *human* to come rushing to our aid? When has he *ever* been reliable? He's still trying to fix the arcane taint that ripped the land open in the *first* place!"

"This will have affected his people, too--"

"Yes, so we can be assured that it will be his *very top* priority," she sneered. "No doubt he'll manage it before his people starve to death." Her mane flared as she shook her head. "The Mage won't be able to help us quickly enough. We must do what *we* can to survive and forget about the rest. We *will not* fall to this."

She moved towards her throne in a graceful fury and swept the ice from the hollow. *'But,'* the thought rose treacherously in the back of her mind as she lowered herself stubbornly upon it, *'how long will it take?'*

Her lip curled in disdain. She had no answer.

So Hlífrún walled the useless voice away.

With a steadying breath and braced jaw, she closed her eyes and melded her spirit with the wood. Like vapour herself, she seeped into the sap, following the tree's veins down into every spidering root, feeling the bite of the frozen soil closing around her though her body remained at the surface. The numbing chill only served to incense her.

Her spirit bled through every hair of the roots and out into the sprawling mykodendrit, then onwards through her domain as fast as the taint itself, tapping into every silvered inch.

And she faced directly the fading light of so many creatures, and the newest gaping chasm in the east.

She allowed herself no time to indulge in the roiling wave of shame that threatened to either drown or freeze her heart. Instead she vowed, directly into the ears of the forests, that she would lead them through it. She had to. Or her reign was meaningless.

She forced her heart to harden and seized the unconscious mind of every other shivering, struggling creature, soothing them, promising that breath would come if they relaxed. The she made her call for aid.

The kvistdjur were to sing and send the most delicate trees to sleep. Näcken were to keep the waters moving. Arkhamas and harpies, once migrants from the south, were ordered to observe the forests and hunt down the humans that were sure to take advantage of the forests' weakness. Stendjur, great stone colossals, were to continue to guard the root bridges, and the vittra were to prevent the approach of hunters and soldiers. Humans would turn to pillaging the forests rather than suffer the chill, especially now, on the brink of hostilities, and she wasn't about to allow an axe to be driven into an open wound.

But their efforts, though honest, wouldn't be enough. The power needed to ensure survival sat upon her own shoulders, and that of the vakehn. And it raked at her heart to know already that that wouldn't be enough, either. Burdens would have to be split, and sacrifice was unavoidable. Those areas that could be lost and regrown would have to be, and their inhabitants moved to safety.

Each such decision moved like a spear through her chest. But she continued to make them.

The forests that could be saved, the vakehn would ward, tending to the more fragile creatures and deterring those allies of the Ghost who would seek to do them more harm. But those few among them with more advanced attunement would work closely beside herself, drawing out the warmth of forest vitality to thaw the land with the heat of life itself.

It was a drastic measure, but it was a drastic situation.

Hlífrún could only hope it would work...

# Vigil

*Ramstead*

The ground was strangely still for evening. Few vibrations rolled through the soil. It was as though only a handful of nocturnal creatures were prowling or digging, despite the arrival of dusk.

Perhaps it was still too light.

The cast of grey throughout the forest was much brighter than usual. The grass was white rather than slate, and the trees were plain against the washed-out depth of shadows. The sky was so intense, it could have had two great, pockmarked discs in it. And against it, the small, drifting pieces of white rain were almost invisible.

They made little more than a whisper as they landed upon the moss-patched boulders. But they held fast. Even when those boulders began to move.

Dust trickled in thin streams as the smallest stones clunked and shifted, then again when larger rocks were dragged into motion. But not one hit the ground. When the largest boulder stirred, the rest clung tightly, fastened by the fungus that bloomed in between, and followed it up onto two stout, stone legs.

Freckled in moss, the limestone colossal stood for a moment in the still, bright evening. White rain continued to settle on its head.

Eventually, it took a slow, heavy, grinding step forwards. Then another. And another. Until its bulk stood at the edge of the only black shape in the forest.

It leaned forwards and peered into the chasm, half as wide as itself was tall. Its black eyes searched the depths. There was nothing to see.

Its attention fell onto the weave of roots that reached from one white clifftop to the other. They were holding strong.

As slowly as it had approached, the stendjur returned to its spot of slate-toned grass, spared from the white by the shelter of its own body, and sat back into a pile of rubble.

Time passed. The sky darkened only a little. White remained

white.

Small vibrations soon moved through the ground. The watchful boulders didn't move.

Two small feet. A little creature - a careful creature - moved quietly through the woods. It stopped here and there, lingered for a while beside a tree, then moved on to repeat the process somewhere else. There was nothing unfamiliar about those feet.

The stendjur soon felt it approach. Such a fragile, puny little thing. It stopped beside the biggest tree, a broad old alder, and placed a dark, dainty hand upon its knotted trunk. It stood there for a while.

Once satisfied, it turned, spared the stendjur a smile, and continued on its way.

Later still, the stendjur rose slowly again, approached the chasm, peered into the depths, peered at the roots, and sat back in the grass.

The white rain became larger. Some pieces were the size of shale. They settled quietly upon its head.

The stendjur rose, approached, peered, and returned once again. The alder, it noticed, was dripping.

The white rain began to thin. The world grew no darker.

The forest was silent.

But something strange disturbed the stendjur's watch.

A jitter rattled through its rocks, slight and meagre, like the early stirrings of a cave-in. But there was no hollow beneath its feet to collapse. It wasn't deep enough to be an earthquake, either. And it couldn't be another of its own kind. It would have noticed.

It lumbered ponderously to its rocky feet, stone grating in its urgency, and stared bewildered into the chasm.

With a sharp little snap, it splintered.

The stendjur jerked in surprise, a stream of dust tumbling from its shoulder. It watched closer in confusion as these newest fractures skittered away into the woods.

Alarm melted through its core.

It seized its first idea.

Heavy feet stamped into the earth over and over and over again, crumbling the ground with each powerful strike. The cracks filled quickly with loosened stone and soil, but they were also hurried along. The chasm's spidering reach spread even further through the forest. They'd grown the length of the stendjur's own towering form by the time it realised its mistake.

The earth quaked again as it crashed urgently to its knees, sending distant birds flying up in a panic, and slammed its great stony fists upon the ground. If filling it wouldn't do, it would simply have to push it all back together. And push it did, with all its might, until the shaking expansion slowed to a halt.

But the colossal didn't let go. Not until one small crack suddenly veered away and darted straight towards a dripping alder tree. A tree it was sure was important.

The splinter widened rapidly, shearing the grey, compacted soil. Long, thick roots were torn free as it passed, left to reach helplessly into the darkness below. Rock and earth continued to fall away around it. The tree had already begun to creak and teeter when the stendjur stomped to its rescue.

With its own jagged mass, it caught the vast trunk upon its back, a cloud of white dust drifting down and vanishing into the dark.

Slowly, the tree stilled, and its roots regained their hold.

But no sooner had the alder been saved than an ash began to topple.

This tree's own roots caught itself at an angle before the stendjur could reach it, but another was already following on the opposite bank. The colossal grasped and pulled that first leaning ash. It caught and propped the other against it.

Then yet another fell.

It was like stones rolling before an avalanche. Despite its efforts, the grey trees continued to fall one by one along the abyss.

Frustration erupted from the stendjur's core.

Its powerful feet stamped deep into the earth, fists thrust into the soil, and it built itself firmly over the chasm. Its gargantuan strength fought to hold the ground in place.

Shards fired out from the darkness. Rocks pulled free by nothing were thrown up into the staggering treetops. One struck the creature's chin, three more its torso. But the stendjur didn't notice them any more than it did the white rain.

Then, they slowed. Then they hung perfectly still among the shining white leaves.

It watched the suspended shards, perplexed as it strained. They didn't move again. So it dismissed them.

The cracks soon stopped widening, and the ground ceased its shake. The chasm finally stilled.

It was a few long moments before the stendjur dared to loosen its hold. Nothing shifted beneath it when it did.

It rose slowly, turning black, empty eyes along the rend. Trees stood at angles, but they were rooted. Nothing was lost.

It turned around and ambled carefully back along the dark splinter, where it stopped and peered over at the bridging mat of roots. They were taut, but whole, and spearing the earth well.

The stendjur rumbled in satisfaction, stepped back, settled into its dark patch of grass, and returned once more to its silent vigil.

# The Kindest Lullaby

*Ellen's Drop*

The crystal morning shattered like glass.

Birds shrieked and scattered at the creaking and splintering of broken twigs, loosing flurries of snow from the branches as panic spread like fire through the white, skeletal trees.

A dark shape swept heedlessly through the falling clouds, its raw, pink face bared to the stinging cold. It moved like a phantom, as though it wasn't there at all, unhindered by the biting frost as its dark cloak billowed, neglected, behind it. But its breath betrayed it, trailing behind as puffs of steam in the crisp morning air.

Booted feet stomped through the snow, snagging on charred roots and catching on stones. But it kept moving forwards. Ever forwards. Through every blunder, every snatch, every stumble; clambering over fallen trees, trampling ash-stained snow, snapping surviving branches as it staggered against them for support. It never stopped moving.

A breeze picked up its voice, whipping it in all directions. It was light, perhaps feminine, but incoherent. And wasted. She was travelling alone.

This human was nothing like the soldiers to the south.


Glowing orange eyes watched cautiously as the figure stumbled into a beech tree. Snow peeled away with her tattered cloak, exposing the burnt bark and agonising memories underneath. The kvistdjur could almost feel the pain all over again, the blinding torment that had seared both the forest and itself – seared *every* kvistdjur connected to this wood. They were bound deep and shared everything. More than just trees had died.

The woman pushed off from it without a glance. She didn't bother to dust herself down. Within moments, she'd disappeared, muttering, into the sloping forest.


What few animals remained in the ruined beechwoods fled from her path, but they, like the shrieks of skríka wrens and the stinging lash of the wind, went unnoticed. Even the low-hanging branches that tangled her hair, and the shrubs that clawed at her sodden robes.

Where the frosted green of life began to edge back in, a foraging jackalope growled and shook its antlers in guard over its unveiled patch of grass. But when she continued to shamble blindly forwards, it yelped and bounded away in a panic.

Where the trees grew fuller and closer, a raghorn pounced as a tawny blur from the blue shadows of the bushes. Its paws planted wide in the snow, muscular shoulders tensed, and its crown of crescent antlers lowered in a sharp and certain threat. But even as it snorted a steaming warning, the woman paid it no heed, tramping on through the sorrel and deadnettle. It snorted again, still to no avail.

It wasted no further warning.

On feline paws, the deer leapt through the snow towards her, moving as fast as an arrow, just as silent, and its antlers just as sharp.

She was saved only by the sudden crackling of light around her.

The raghorn turned and bolted.

Small flickers like violent fireflies popped and flashed in the air by her head, growing steadily to the size of her fists as she staggered and clutched desperately at her hair. Like compressed thunder, the air snapped with each burst, and her fevered muttering swelled into pleading sobs as she collapsed to her knees. Her body rocked back and forth, knuckles as white as the snow.

Glowing orange eyes watched vigilantly over the phantom struggle.

Slowly, very slowly, the crackling lights thinned until the air fell still once more, muffled by the snow into bleak silence but for her grievous weeping.

Until something else snared her urgency.

She staggered suddenly back to her feet, the strange, distant glaze returning to her eyes, and stumbled onwards as though nothing had happened, muttering all the while.

The kvistdjur had seen this before. Humans tainted by their own magic. Maddened by it.

A sorely familiar danger - a danger that would only end one way.

And she would take a swathe of the forest, countless kvistdjur, and all their charges with her.

The glowing orange eyes narrowed as they tracked her through the trees.

The sky grew darker as the morning aged. No sun reached the surviving leaves nor melted their entombment, and the breeze that rustled through them was brutal. The woman had begun to slow and falter, caught at last by fatigue. Her stumbling had become a lurch, and when the forest or her own boots tripped her, she took longer to find her feet. Yet still, she moved forwards.

The wildlife here did not flee as she reeled through. Instead they watched her with dark eyes from branches, knot-holes and black river waters. Those that remained here, so close to human destruction, had no choice in the matter. They were tied to their homes. And the woman was an intruder.

Hands, both scaled and twiggy, reached out from water and tree to snare her in their insult, but none succeeded in any more than a torn piece of fabric or handful of falling snow. The moment of shock and fright that would stall any other human and seal their fate never came. She walked on, unaware.

She didn't hear the beautiful violinic voices that sought to lure her to the water's edge, nor see the shimmering white stallions that pranced deceitfully along the banks. She didn't smell the delicate fragrance of warm, split berries that rose above even the numbing cold, nor feel the unseen hand that would lead her merrily to the darkest caves.

Every trick was lost upon her.

The opening of an abandoned warren, hidden beneath the snow, finally sent her to her knees. She tried to rise, but fell again. She gave up after a second attempt and crawled onwards instead, forcing her way through the bushes, crooked ankle dragging along behind her. She ignored it just as she did the bitter, biting chill of the snow against her bare hands, and the twigs that scratched her cheeks, lips and eyes.

A swathe of light cut through a sudden opening in the trees. The muffled luminance that bounced between cloud and snow cast a brilliance into the forest's narrow, open vein. It was here that she finally collapsed.

The woods fell silent. Her muttering had ceased.

Crows leaned forwards from their dusty perches. A few swept down, venturing a closer look at the still form, while a few hopped within the reach of a daring beak. One soon tugged experimentally at the dark cloak that spilled around her. Others joined in when she didn't move.

Only when one began to peck at the wounds across her bloodied cheek did she finally stir, sending them flying in a noisy panic as she forced herself up from the crimson-flecked snow and sat huddled in a ball.

She began to weep.

She could go no further.

The chasm in the earth before her was one of the widest in the country. This northernmost border had been shattered long ago, and the snow-shrouded roots that stitched it were not fit to cross.

But, she didn't try.

Glowing orange eyes watched her impassively.

She had arrived. The magic hummed in the air here, the very cause of the rend itself. And she, like so many others of her afflicted kind, were fatally drawn to it.

The kvistdjur didn't have to wait long for its chance.

Before the hidden sun could reach its zenith, a calmness gathered around her. Her weeping weakened and faded, the air about her slowed, and her life force quietened to a whisper.

She was asleep.

She would have no chance to attack. No chance to panic. No chance to destroy herself nor the forest with her. No chance to understand what her own magic was doing to her.

No chance to feel any pain.

It was the kindest thing. For everyone. She had less than an hour left.

The kvistdjur stepped away from the trees. In a heartbeat, it was beside her, raising its wooden talons. Its orange firefly eyes flared with duty.

# Fragments and Remnants

*Hagstone Woods*

Rose-gold light glittered as it trickled through the frost-feathered gaps in the trees. The frozen silence of the oakwoods floated wherever it glowed, evaporating its hold over the crisp morning air, and thin ribbons of cautious birdsong had finally begun to weave through the boughs. The dawn chorus was late again, but at least, today, it had come.

Beneath the graceful shapes of birds flitting through the morning beams, the snow rounded everything like a carpet of white moss. Cast in azure shadows, crystal leaves drooped lazily over a creek of amber water, flowing strong and flecked with small fish despite the grasp of the cold. The same blushing glow shimmered across the icicles clinging to the edges of gentle falls, and bounced across the stones of an ancient ruin, long reclaimed by the wilds.

All appeared calm, patient and beautiful in the embrace of the snow.

But it was all false.

The soft gold of the rising sun was impossible to distinguish from the rich hues of sunset, where shrouds of dusk itself cocooned the smallest pieces of masoned stone. Birdsong was laced with the faintest melody, a discordant tune that drifted in from nowhere, reminiscent of something dreadful and near-forgotten. And the trees, sparkling in the morning light, had been pulled and shattered into pieces. Fragmented trunks hung suspended in the air, connected only by the brace of icicles that inched through the grooves in their bark.

The ruin, of course, fared better. The snow only softened its weathered features, and the two surviving pillars were in tact. It stood oblivious, consumed instead with self-pity for the ravaging of time, even as the earth around it swelled and deflated as slowly as a colossal beast breathing in its sleep.

Hlífrún watched contemptuously as the earth rose impossibly yet again.

One...two...three...four...and a half.

It lowered again.

One...two...three...four...five...and a quarter.

It rose.

Another four-and-a-half count, and it deflated once more.

She snarled, tightening the steadying fold of her arms. "*Foul magic.*"

Her eyes snapped away as her anger swelled even higher, and panned across the pocket of artificial beauty that further spoiled this particular frozen corner of her domain. But the harsh twist of her lips softened when she spotted the thin, intermittent shadow of tiny tracks in the ground.

She stepped back into the nearest tree, melted into the bark, and reappeared from another overlooking the trail. Peering closer at the light prints and the small ruffles of scuffed snow, she smiled. She'd felt no life here but that of the suffering trees, and had thought that the creatures that called it home had died. So many others had, the smallest especially, and in places as infected as this, the magic all too often trapped their minds or changed their bodies. How many, she wondered, had even noticed something was wrong before the magic had killed them?

These voles had, whatever the case. They'd been lucky. How lucky, though, she didn't have the heart to find out. She chose not to follow the tracks.

Her attention shifted back onto the ruin, and her eyes darkened violently yet again.

This place had been abandoned over a millennia ago - all the thousands of places built deep within the forests or mountains had been. Abandoned when the people of that age had decided themselves better than the world that birthed them and left it behind, building themselves opulent and unnatural environments on the plains from the world's very bones instead.

And now, these long-forgotten blemishes were reviving. Sodden with fragments of magic that escaped civilisation's attention, they were transforming into springs of raw power that took just one agitation to detonate. And it was *her* domain that was suffering for it, *her* kin being corrupted and destroyed, while the guilty kept a safe distance and continued their indulgence.

And yet, she was all too painfully aware that the lure that drew the magic here was as natural and insurmountable as its consequences.

Her jaw tightened as she stepped out from the tree. The snow's chill went unnoticed. It had become as constant as the air.

Cautiously, she approached the stone platform, the louring magic swirling closer around her with each careful stride. It grew tighter as she reached the foot of the sunset-wrapped steps, and with its loathsome grasp came that same ominous presence, seeping through reality like blood through water. The same presence she'd felt at every other ruin. The presence of those that had naively unleashed this magic upon the world in the first place. And of those that had given her her crown.

She drew to a careful stop at the top of the steps. A crumbled, snow-rounded altar stood at the centre beneath the arch. Her back tightened, bark-hollow contracting with it. Her tail flicked uneasily.

The realm of the gods felt dark...

Time stood still as she lingered, staring into nothing. Her mind ticked away with questions she doubted They would ever answer, if she would ever ask them. Slowly, her toned shoulders rounded, and her heart began to wilt.

Impotence clamped around her like a carpenter's vice.

A bitter wind snatched her suddenly back to the ruins, minutes or seconds later, rustling through the leaves. For a single, blissful moment, she didn't hear the ice that limned their edges. For a single, blissful moment, the forest was as it should have been.

She closed her eyes to preserve the instant, blocking out the cold, the white, the dissonant melody that persisted where the birds had ceased.

Until a voice growled from deep within her bones.

Her eyes opened again, and stared back into that sovereign presence.

She stood before her Mother as a fool.

The bleak aura of the gods had thickened. She felt it creep up over her, the judgement, the pressure, the doubt. Even though she knew Feira wasn't one to evoke fear, *especially* from her.

But, *shame*...

Hlífrún bit off a snarl and forced her back to straighten, puffing her chest proudly. She wouldn't give in to shame. She'd prove herself worthy of her position, and she'd serve Feira to her final, dying breath, whenever or however it may come.

She whirled sharply, a white flurry kicking up about her feet, and stormed back down the steps. The slowly heaving snow crunched beneath her strides.

The magic - the sunsets, the music, the fragmentation - she could do nothing against. Not herself, nor the vakehn, as versed in magic as they were, all because it was the wrong breed. But others who could, they would certainly try - for better or for worse.

Which left her only one solution for these time-lost places.

She returned to her place among the crystal trees and looked back out across the long-forgotten shrine to the Goddess of Nature. With resentment, with sorrow, she slammed her woody palm down through the snow and into the frozen soil, where her fingers melded with the fibrous mykodendrit beneath.

Almost immediately, the trees began to stir, creaking, cracking and tinkling in showers of frost. All around the overgrown clearing, roots crept out through the snow, reaching up into the cold, stretching higher and further, lacing together in a wooden tangle. Branches, too, reached down and tied their frostbitten arms into the weave.

After the thump of nine tense heartbeats, the creaking stilled, and a gnarled, wooden wall towered around the clearing. With its foundations deep, its reach as high as the tallest boughs, and haunted by the spirits still bound to those trees, it would not be an obstacle easily passed.

But, while it would keep others out, it wouldn't keep the magic in.

Hlífrún withdrew her hand from the fungal web and rose silently to her feet, watching the ground's slow, heaving breath through the weave.

She restrained the tormented sigh. There was little satisfaction to be found in this solution. It was a delay, at best. But it was all she could do.

Heavy-hearted, she turned away and stepped back into the nearest tree. There was more that needed tending than this.

The glare of the snow was blinding. There were no trees here to break up the landscape, nor hide the dark, leaden sky. But she spared no notice to the inversion of the light across the ivory moors, nor the falling shadows of broad flakes that thickened the smothering blanket.

She stepped out from the shrub, its fruits trapped within a shell of ice, and stormed her way through the snow, her lip curling in disgust with every wretched crunch. Over the past ten days, the cold, the sound, the numbing absence of smell had only made her increasingly irascible, and the sight of such a vast spread threatened to split her bark even deeper if her sap ran any hotter. Though, she was at least spared the usual discomfort that came from the exposure of the open fields.

Such emptiness unsettled most of her kin. Only the vittra dared venture through it to graze their cattle, so much like humans they appeared, if a little smaller and weasel-featured. The rest felt unwelcome, convinced that, if they were seen for even a moment, humans would attack them in a heartbeat. And they were usually right.

But this was no time for anxiety. Hlífrún could tear apart any human with as much ease as a bear - and these grasses and flowers were as much her charge as the forests. Everywhere the mykodendrit spread was her responsibility, and had been long before 'civilisation' reared its wasteful, destructive head.

And this chasm, as wide as the height of the tallest tree, as black as a shard of polished obsidian, needed bridging just like the others. Or she would lose her entire hold over Doana and the east.

She controlled her roiling fury as best she could as she walked along its length, and stopped as she reached a copse of trees, sheared in two but still standing. There, she knelt, and merged once more with the network. Slowly, the frigid roots began to stir and grow to her will.

The muscles between her bare, grey shoulders knotted as she worked, and the furrow in her brow deepened. Her toes lengthened and burrowed into the ground, rooting her down when she began to waver. She hadn't slept in days. But there was too much to do to waste time.

Since this taint had stormed in, she'd been working in a constant state of emergency. Between bridging these chasms, she and her vakehn had been warming the forests - a slow and exhausting process that had started experimentally at first, then quickly applied across the country. But Ramstead had been only mildly affected, and the trees there were dense already, and the kvistdjur prolific. They hadn't sung those trees to sleep, but invigorated them, and, alongside her efforts, had began to thaw the snow. But the only other regions likely to follow so easily were her throne's Wildlands in the east, and Korovor to the north. Not all trees and plants could produce the same degree of heat. The rest would take far longer.

But it was all they could do. Anything to prevent the synaptic network from freezing or withering.

And all that while confronting the rest of human threat: greed, aggression, and hate, even overlooking those magic-wielders who had been poisoned by their own blood and driven mad to the point of self-destruction. Because now, even just the simplest hunters had become a problem. They'd always moved through the forests, and she'd tolerated it - but now they were moving deeper into places usually too wild for the wise to risk, and old customs were being forgotten. And when the old customs died, respect and fear went with them. They were being blinded by desperation, consumed by the need to survive, and no longer gave any thought to what else might be struggling in the shadows beside them.

Those with nothing but starving families could be forgiven for that - but so could her creatures.

Their threat made it a bud in need of nipping before either side could go too far, before there was too little to go around, and before the wilds lost the protection their mystery provided. The vakehn had been put to work on that - and the good-natured vittra had proposed another measure, too, if just to avoid bloodshed on either side. She'd accepted it, grudgingly, but it had yet to bear fruit.

For now, hunters were a frequent but growing nuisance.

And remained only the simplest of her problems.

War had been brewing for months, and soldiers from both sides had made themselves comfortable in a few of the forests. Most had their own food reserves, but inevitably the petty creatures attempted to foil the others by inconveniencing them, and then they turned to wild game, too. And when they, in their numbers, encountered anything strange or defensive along their way, they were quick to attack it. They were always *so* brave when they outnumbered a beast six-to-one.

For fun, they would break branches and twigs, trample and vandalise, drink, shout and sing. They would light large, careless fires, they would kill beasts for food, always far more than they needed, and gather other creatures' forage though the animals were already struggling.

Yes. They were also being dealt with. She looked forward to the moment they finally attacked directly and killed one another.

She raised her head and stared with burning eyes across the expanse, watching the roots reach slowly across the void.

But even the soldiers were not the worst of them. No, the worst of humans were the sneaks. Those who slipped into the woods unseen. Those who came in to kill. Always. To deliberately kill her kin, and sometimes others. Others who would actually do *good*.

Their prey among her kin were the Arkhamas and the harpies. *Such* a terrible menace they were, the clothes-stealing half-children and the quietly roosting birds, and *certainly* the only 'strange' things living in the woods. They didn't expect more than the occasional raghorn.

And so they were never prepared for the ferocity of a kvistdjur or the reaching hand of an askafroa, nor certainly the deceptive magic of the vakehn - magic that played upon the mysteries of the wilds: the figures of shadows, confusion of fog, displaced echoes, roots and hollows hidden beneath leaf litter.

No. These were the worst of humans. Those who moved like ghosts, those with no vestige of anything good left in them, warped by the gluttony of their world, shaped into living weapons to achieve it, who would turn nature against nature, who would burn and flood forests and destroy their prey and everything else with it. Those who would kill even their own kind on a single order.

The very worst of their species. And the hardest to handle.

But now her forests were organised. With their every attack over this past month, her kin had grown vigilant. And now, all eyes were working together. They would continue to sneak in, but they certainly wouldn't be missed.

The roots speared slowly into the opposite cliff.

Her attention beneath the soil slipped from root to fungus, and the off-white, fibrous web immediately sprouted from both sides of the sheared soil and creep their way across the roots.

As much trouble as the humans were, as frustrating as their damage was, she had to regain as much control as possible. Because these were *her* lands, and without her, there would be no wood for their fires, no honey for their breakfast, no wheat for their bread nor meat on their table.

She would make sure they came to respect the wilds. And they would fear her again.

The survival of nature itself was in her hands, and she would not fail Feira now.

*Eighteen days.*

A deep, groaning rumble broke the eternal stillness of the Pavise Mountains.

The silent spruce slopes erupted into a clamour of whoops, howls and screeches as alarm spread like wildfire.

Alpine lemurs fled the shaking trees, snow falcons abandoned their hunts, bears gathered their cubs and deserted their dens.

But the rumble was not of avalanches barrelling through the pines.

The bones of the mountains shook as magic carved its way through solid rock, stretching the chasm by sheer power alone, felling uncountable trees, collapsing ancient towers and shrines, tumbling ahead like a raging torrent, falling over itself in zeal.

It slipped at random through the western reach and down into the lower fells. Grey stone gave way to green as it traced the weakest lines in the earth. It latched into an old water trail, the bed more easily cut, and followed the canyon of limestone and moss like blood along the edge of a knife.

It sundered a village carved into the canyon face. Collapsed a shrine built into the fork. Rent open hides and hovels secreted in the rocks. Nothing was incorruptible. Nothing was exempt.

Nothing could slow it down.

# Chapter 7

A mottle of grey and green opened up across the plain. The tidy arrangement of round and jagged rocks were painted with shades that seemed meticulously applied to complement. Every patch of grass and moss that found a hold even on the ancient canyon's sheerest face appeared both softer and lusher, while the rock itself seemed more robust, quiet and stoic. It was the perfect interruption to the sprawling, featureless meadow.

There was no snow here, either; the magic had thinned out on the near side of the White River. This far west, grass still grew, carpeting patches of the canyon, while above hung the clear and eager moon as daylight faded leisurely into dusk.

But the comfort in that was thin.

Hlífrún watched from a distance as yet more stone crumbled away from the cliff at the fork. Another larger fragment fell free, and dragged with it another piece of the old earthen shrine lying beneath. They both vanished into the black scar that had ripped through the old river bed.

A sigh of ever-increasing heartache passed her lips before the warm, summer wind snatched it away.

This canyon had always been a difficult area, but a vital one. The soil was thin and too deficient to support anything but grass, and that in turn stunted her network. But this one-hundred-mile natural hardship was its only extension into Skilan and Kalokh, and her single link to the west. And now it, too, was sundered. What fragile hold it had was broken.

She should have seen it coming. She should have reinforced it, safeguarded it somehow. But she hadn't had the chance. Even had she thought of it, the wretched snow and the shattering of the eastern borders had consumed her attention. And neither of those events could have been predicted.

Her lips twitched into a sickened grimace.

Now, at least, in some twisted fortune, there was nothing left to try to foresee. The borders had all been split. Turunda had been broken from the rest of the continent to a mile or more beneath the soil.

The damage had been done, and now she had to contain it; re-establish her reach into the west while the wounds were still fresh, before the sap could harden, the roots could wither, and the network could shrivel and die.

She took a step backwards through the soft grass and immediately began to shrink. Her grey, bark-like skin smoothed and lightened, brightening to green as she vanished among the blades.

She reappeared again at the bottom of the canyon, emerging from one of the few dwarf trees that had managed to take root in a shallow pocket of soil. The stunted thing wasn't up to the task, but it had to do. She set to work bridging the chasm in silence while some of the surrounding grass blackened in sacrifice.

The struggle would have made her sick had she not been so furious.

She rose back to her feet when the task was done, just as a boulder began to shift and grate behind her. Her voice cracked like a broken branch. But this was no magic. *'Trolls. Wonderful.'*

She didn't slip back into the exhausted tree. She straightened instead, empowering her bearing, and made no attempt at all to conceal the irritated flick of her tail. Sure enough, moments later, a tall, sturdy figure appeared alongside her. The earthy scent of dust and damp hung almost pleasantly around him, but it was far from enough to evoke even the shadow of a smile.

"Evening," he grunted sedately, even as he peered out along the chasm that opened just a step away from his bare feet. He shook his balding head with the slightest tut. "Quite a mess."

"Regrettably."

He gestured towards the roots with his large, hooked nose. "Not strong enough to cross?"

"Not if you don't want twigs growing out of your eyes."

"Mm," he scratched his chin thoughtfully. "Can't say that I do."

Hlífrún made some effort to stifle her irritation. It wouldn't do to incite the trolls. They may not have been creatures of the forest, nor did they answer to her reign, but they were sparing in their use of resources, and a good many took it upon themselves to guard certain areas of wilds even beyond the boundaries of their own homes. She wanted to keep it that way.

She felt his green eyes slip onto her at last, his long, flat pupils widening. She knew what was coming.

"Will this take long?" He looked back along the chasm when she failed to reply. "You don't know."

"I'm doing all I can."

"I have no doubt," he grunted. "But is it enough?"

"It has to be."

The two stood in a polite and irksome silence for a moment, the moon growing brighter in the slowly darkening sky. Finally, the troll moved, shifting his bulky weight and shaking his head once more, breathing a withering sigh. "Humans. The younger races are always troublesome. Yet it seems to get worse the older they get."

"Wisdom doesn't come to us all."

"It does, if circumstances are dire enough."

"This should *be* dire enough!" She hissed. But her venom slipped over the troll.

"It may well be, eventually," he replied with his usual mild stoicism. "But, if it isn't...someone should be tackling the cause."

"Someone is."

His gaze crashed back onto her. It was the first thing to break his quiet expression since he'd arrived. Hlífrún hid that small spike of satisfaction.

He turned back out to the chasm, composure slipping back in. "Then good luck to her."

"Him."

He grunted. "Yours are usually 'her'. Makes little difference to me, though. So long as he can put a stop to it, he could be a bit of both or neither for all I care. But I wonder: will the world still be standing when he does?"

Her satisfaction was fleeting. She whipped towards him with another poisonous hiss. "What are you implying?"

"It's no use taking your frustration out on me. None of it is my fault."

"Yet you stand there passing judgement without lifting a finger to help, yourself."

He simply spread his dirty hands. "What could I do that you cannot? If you have a suggestion, please make it, and I will see it done."

She snapped away in a huff. He was right, of course.

The grunt of conceit she'd expected never came. "Should that

55

change," he said instead, "the offer stands. I am always willing to help. I don't wish to see this world die, either."

They both turned at the sound of gentle footsteps. A young woman stood in the cave opening beside the shifted rock, a beautiful girl, as most troll maidens were, if her features were slightly lopsided. She curtseyed deeply towards Hlífrún, then gave her father a polite but beckoning look.

"Well, whatever the case," he concluded, stepping towards his daughter, "I'm certain you'll manage it. You've done something similar before." He followed her back into their home in the rockface, and cast Hlífrún a deep, honest bow in the doorway. "Pleasure, 'Majesty."

She inclined her head as he pulled the rock rather effortlessly back in place, but her expression remained vexed. The moment the door had closed, she stepped back into the trunk of the tree.

The troll had spoken the truth. Bluntly, as he and his kin so often did. It was why she disliked them. And while she knew she was being petty, she was in no mood to correct herself.

She still had too much to do.

# The Hunted

*Hoarwood*

"I'd advise against going in there."

He watched the cloaked figure jump at his voice and squint anxiously through the fire towards him. The man's eyes were wide with terror.

He frowned, confused, until he realised his thick red scarf still covered most of his face. He must have looked like a bandit, albeit one waiting in the open light of a fire. But night did funny things to people's minds.

He pulled it down and smiled. The man returned it nervously. "'Tis a thick wood," he continued, nodding towards the forest behind him. "And besides that, there's strange goings-on. Could be wildlings. Could be magic." He looked at the cloaked man a little more closely. He'd come in from the north, and had, by the sodden hem of his cloak, avoided the road for some time. "Are you travelling?"

"Oh, yes - to Roeden."

"Roeden, eh?" He waved him closer to the fire. The man obliged uneasily. "In that case, I'd also advise that you find another way. Take the Western Loop instead. It'll add a couple of days to your journey, but it's safer than venturing through Hoarwood right now. Here," he lifted a wrapped and tied-off bundle from his bag and offered it towards him. "This will tide you over."

"Oh...that's very kind of you..."

"Yes, it is. But the world could use a little more kindness these days. Don't you agree?" He waved the package encouragingly. But the man, a moment ago so doubtful, now simply smiled.

"Certainly. So I can't take it."

"Of course you can take it."

"No, thank you, sir," he replied quite assuredly, "I'll be fine. I've packed plenty." He patted the clattering bag beneath his cloak. "You can't be too sure in this strange sort of weather."

"No, I suppose not...well, the sun will rise in an hour or two -

would you care to sit for a while? Some milk?" He offered up a yak skin, but the cloaked man was already waving it off and stepping around the modest camp.

"No, thank you. I should be getting along. The Western Loop is an hour away - the sooner I set off, the sooner I arrive." He inclined his head with a smile and pulled his cloak a little closer. "Thank you for the advice, friend." And with that, he resumed his journey through the early hours of the morning, making now towards the west.

The red-scarfed man shrugged and turned back to his fire.

And the traveller dashed quickly into the trees.

His foot caught immediately in the thick bramble. Head over heels he tumbled until he struck a knotted tree trunk, and managed, somehow, to stifle his shock behind his lips. He was quick to scramble back to his feet, and hurried onwards with only a few brief glances back over his shoulder, but there was no sight nor sound of the red-scarfed man. In fact, the forest seemed to have closed around him.

His feet slowed as he looked about himself, and he soon appeared to remember something, for he took a moment to pause and almost physically seize his bearings. It was far darker within the woods, and ominous, even despite the snow. Surely he must have felt that something was off. The snow, after all, wasn't as thick as it was outside. But he'd probably just hastily concluded that the crown was simply thicker than it seemed and put the thought out of his mind. He wouldn't want to be in the forest any longer than he needed to be, either way.

So he trudged on, pulling his cloak tighter about himself as though it offered the same protection as a soldier's shield, and down lower over his bag, too, which was clearly a small and poorly hidden bow and quiver. He negotiated carefully through another patch of brambles, trying to place his feet more quietly against the dense silence, and swatted absently at the stripe-winged butterfly that fluttered persistently in front of his face.

The fellow had the look of a family man. His face was furrowed by lines equal parts frown and smile, his hands were scarred, rough skin tanned from a hard job, his clothes were well-patched by a loving wife, and, most obviously, a desperation haunted his tired eyes.

That, and a small teddy was secured tightly to his belt - a good-luck charm pressed upon him by his eldest, no doubt.

So he'd ventured into the dense tangles of Hoarwood to look for food. But there was something he had to do first.

He veered onto the small, trampled route often taken by his kinsmen and followed it to the flat old tree stump, still spotted with blood from offerings made generations ago. Fortunately, most deemed those kinds of offerings out-dated and, unbeknownst to them, the forest denizens agreed - but dues of one kind or another were still expected to be paid.

He reached beneath his cloak as he arrived. And then he cursed, quiet but vehemently. After patting himself down several times, he cursed again. He must have forgotten the offering.

He stood for a tense moment before turning and walking back along the trail, his back rigid and fists tight as he told himself, most likely, that he didn't need to make an offering of a handful of coins or a lump of cheese to what was nothing more than a superstition.

It was clear from the hesitation in his footing and his backward glances that he didn't really believe that.

Even at this hour, there were far fewer noises in the forest than there should have been for midsummer. But, even so, there still seemed to be enough to rip the occasional squeak from the man. Before long, he resorted to drawing his bow and loosely nocking an arrow for comfort.

It was both quickly and woefully clear that he wasn't a proficient hunter. Despite his efforts, he stepped too loudly, moved too sharply, he wasn't listening for anything but danger, and his arrow, should he pull it tight, would have been positioned just one third along the length of the string.

Clearly, he was desperate.

He swatted again at the butterfly.

That wasn't helping matters. They certainly knew better, but the young weren't keen to hang back. Patience had never been a value of youth.

It took some time for anything to stir the hunter's attention beyond jumping at shadows or the distant, mournful lament rolling through the forest, until a jackalope finally appeared, chewing crunchy, frozen berries just off from the narrow boar trail. The hefty creatures were abundant in most woods, but they were as quick to flee as they were to attack. They weren't reliable prey. A proficient hunter would have known that.

True to form, the antlered rabbit vanished before he could raise his bow.

The next opportunity came in the shape of a deer. But he wasn't aware of its presence until it bounded past him. He was lucky that was a doe – and luckier still that its feet ended in hooves. A raghorn would have made a much greater effort to gore him. But, again, it was gone before he had the chance to draw.

Three weasels scurried away into a log as soon as he stepped into the small clearing, and he immediately set to trying to lure them out with the frozen berries the jackalope had abandoned. But they weren't so foolish as to let themselves be coaxed out, and a nearby shriek in the darkness discouraged him from lingering long enough to outsmart them.

But he moved more quietly now, finally learning from his mistakes, and soon came upon a covey of wood grouse. They didn't flee. Though that wasn't necessarily down to his own efforts.

He stopped quietly, stooping low in the undergrowth almost as an after-thought, and drew back his bow. He took a long moment to adjust his hold on the string, and just as he had it, three more striped butterflies quickly swept in and began fluttering feverishly in his face. He swept his bow around at them. They couldn't be blamed for this urgency, but now that this desperate father had found a target, they couldn't possibly do a thing to discourage him.

He gave up on them, quite rightly, and loosed his arrow into the flock. The butterflies looped away in a panic.

But of course the arrow didn't hit. The fair Root Mother had thin patience with humans these days, and measures had been taken to ease her fractious moods.

The arrows bounced off of thin air.

He breathed a flustered grunt and quickly drew again, loosing it with even less control than the first. But, this time, it would have made no difference even *had* he been a proficient hunter. Once more, the arrow ricocheted off of nothing at all.

The young butterflies swept back in, but this time his frantic movements to shoo off their assault caught the covey's notice, and the birds fled in all directions, squawking through the bushes.

He bit off a sharp curse and leapt to his feet, chasing them clumsily through the dense tangle.

It was a trial to keep up with him, but, fortunately, humans were grounded creatures, and the cacophony of snapping twigs and stifled yelps from thorns scratching his face and hands made it difficult to lose him.

When he finally stopped, he'd long lost sight of the birds. He stood puffing and panting great clouds of vapour, fighting against the chill to reclaim his breath. When he finally recovered enough to stand up straight, he began looking about himself wildly until he was all but spinning around on the spot. It wasn't particularly fair, the forest *had* moved to confuse him, but it had no desire to *trap* him. Not yet, anyway.

Regrettably, at this point, the only thing to do was hang back and let him panic. Hunting was no longer at the forefront of the man's mind.

Shadows flickered, the motion of a glancing breeze. He spun towards it. Then jumped again at the sound of a passing bird. Then at the muffled thump of snow from an over-loaded branch.

Very quickly, every noise and movement began to spook him. It didn't take him long to start stumbling back through the forest at break-neck speed.

He snatched himself to a stop every few moments and spun around, looking for markers he would never have spotted in his approach anyway, before hurtling feverishly onwards once again. The forest clawed at him as he passed, a trick of the mind on the part of the trees, but less so by the twiggy hand of a malicious askafroa. The snow, though thin by the vakehn's efforts, still lay within the woods and cast a ghostly pallor throughout the surroundings, at least to the poor hunter's eye. And with the moonlight blocked out, and the rise of another kvistdjur's lullaby, there was little to illuminate or dispel his horror.

The time had come.

A red-striped butterfly fluttered down from the heights.

The hunter moved to bat it away, but as yet another unfamiliar knot of groping trees loomed in his path, something stilled his hand. Desperation, certainly; some hope that perhaps such a delicate creature wouldn't or couldn't hurt him. There were, after all, no stories about butterflies leading men to their deaths.

But there were no stories of them helping any, either.

But, while this one floated sedately at just the right distance, deliberately near yet just out of reach, curiosity began to elbow its way past his fright. He still hesitated, though, when it fluttered a short distance into the trees and then back again. It took three more suggestions before the man looked dismally about himself one last time. He still seemed unable to recognise anything.

Finally, he took a slow, cautious step forwards at the butterfly's fifth pass, and followed it uncertainly into the undergrowth.

Shadows and noises, and even creatures who truly were lurking nearby, frequently stole his fraying attention, but the butterfly reclaimed his focus by fluttering quickly back into his eyes. Their pace picked up when a shriek rose sharply from behind them. At a second and much closer cry, he began to run. At the third, the man was in tears, and struck the snow hard as his boot caught on something hidden in the growth.

He scrambled back up immediately and rushed on, until he discovered nothing but clear snow ahead. The nearest tree was a speck on the twilight horizon.

He staggered to a stop. His shock was plain in his watery eyes. He didn't trust it, but his heart overpowered his mind. And this time, it was right to. He'd probably not felt such relief in a very long time - perhaps not even since he was a child and had escaped some imagined creature. Or *not*-so-imagined creature.

His wide gaze travelled slowly onto the butterfly that perched upon a rock beside him. A smooth, pale rock, free from snow, and tied with a length of twine.

It looked remarkably like the package the man at the campfire had offered him.

The butterfly flew off into the trees, forgotten as he reached for the bundle, and he quickly pulled loose the string. Inside the linen lay a brace of rabbits, fresher than the finest hunter's market stall, a selection of vegetables, and a strange collection of off-white mushrooms, each with multiple heads on a single slender stalk.

The hunter stared at first in disbelief at the bounty, then dubiety.

He tentatively lifted one of those mushrooms, which itself had small, tangled fibres about its base, and sniffed it. He paused, uncertain, but when his empty stomach finally rumbled, he answered the compulsion and bit off a small piece.

His eyes brightened immediately.

Apparently convinced by the sweet taste of burnt caramel, he quickly devoured the rest of the stalk and tied the package back up, tucked his bow beneath his cloak, and ran off into the night without a backwards look.

The red-scarfed vittra watched him from his perch in the tree branches with a smile of satisfaction.

# Obsession

## *The Ghost Patch*

The black eyes of a woodpecker peered about in cautious habit as it landed upon the ash tree. There was no movement in the silver forest, no sign of anything. No competition, no predators. It was a perfectly safe, perfectly quiet morning, with still plenty of foraging.

Encouraged, it hopped up and around the trunk, gripping the bark with long, hooked talons, before finally settling on a high spot on the north side, and assessed the best place to start boring.

A small, slender branch lowered slowly down towards it.

The woodpecker noticed just before the twiggy fingers could close.

The bird fled with a panicked rasp, leaving the hand to snatch at the empty spot while a gaunt, grey face burst out through the branches and hissed venomously after it.

*Wicked pest!*

Behind the fading flap of its wings, the forest fell still and silent once again.

The askafroa stared hatefully through the morning from her branch, searching the blue shadows with dark, speckled eyes. This wouldn't be the last time she shooed the wretched thing off, no, no. Birds were drawn to her tree. They knew it would make a sturdy home, or a fine rummaging ground, covered in worms and grubs and beetles. But there were none in this cold! They would only rip the bark, and if they weren't removing pests, they were nothing but a nuisance!

She slipped deeper into the branches, grasped one as she passed and shook it violently, freeing its leaves from the frost.

*Not me. Not my tree.*

She clambered around its trunk as efficiently as a squirrel and made her usual check of the bark, stopping every few minutes to lash out at yet more foolish birds that tried to land as blindly upon her head as they did upon the branches. Yes, yes, she was quite nearly invisible - her skin matched the bark and the lichen perfectly, and it frosted the same way, while her limbs and long ears uncannily resembled twigs, and even her hair appeared like a tangle of moss and spider silk. But she *moved*, while the tree did not. Surely the birds could tell the difference!

Once satisfied that the bark wasn't suddenly peeling, infested or burning, she scurried up into the heights and shook off more of the relentless frost, sending a gentle, tinkling rustle through the forest - which had the added perk of discouraging at least a few more of the pesky creatures. Then she retreated into the depths of the trunk and reached down below the roots, searching for any sumptuous waterways that had yet to freeze solid.

Footsteps broke the silence. She hissed from the trunk and watched indignantly through the branches as a hide-clad vakah walked by. He was irritatingly calm, and smiled up at her as he stopped at the foot of her dear tree. She didn't smile back. Then he dared to place his hand upon it.

She rose from her crouch and hissed again, making herself bigger, baring her sharp teeth. But he didn't withdraw. Didn't withdraw at all.

*I don't need your help!*

And yet, neither did she lash out. Within moments, something passed through the sap, and she felt suddenly rejuvenated. A vitality she only now realised she'd been missing.

She maintained her threatening stance when the vakah removed his hand and smiled once again, and watched the brazen thing closely as he walked away.

Only once his presence had vanished did she melt back into the branches, chittering irritably to herself, to finish her chores.

Then began her longest task.

Sitting silently in the shadows of the leaves, she dropped deep into the lifeblood of the tree, made herself quite comfortable, and listened attentively to the slow whisper of the soil.

It had become harder to hear anything since the white death had rolled in. Many trees had been killed, many, and the soils were slower to talk. And there was a lot to be aware of. Mostly, the humans that stomp-stomp-stomped through the woods, cutting down tree after tree after tree to burn in their homes, or scorching them where they stood. Or drowning them, as they had not all that far to the south.

She hissed quietly to herself.

*Wretched creatures. Pointless creatures.*

They had become arrogant. Bold. Brazen! The usual measures were no longer fitting; no curses or sicknesses would solve this problem. Any who passed within her reach would be snatched, be they hunter or soldier; leather or shiny steel. They would be dragged up into her tree, their necks would be wrung, and their bodies would feed the woods, and feed the woods well.

*Not me. Not my tree. I will not let my tree fall.*

No, no, none of her kind would. They were bound - an ash tree was an askafroa's life, and an askafroa the tree's. She would lose more than her home if humans managed to get their fat, sticky, fleshy fingers on it. And if her actions in its defence happened to fill Rötternas Moder's commands, then it was coincidence and nothing more. Nothing more at all.


Her eyes flashed open to the night. All was still, all was silent. There were no birds to pester her. She'd chased them off all throughout the day.

Instead, something was stirring in the soil.

She sank a little deeper, peering inside, listening closer, fixing on its location. Something slowly began to take shape.

A warning.

In that moment, she started to notice vibrations, stretching through the ground from the north-east. Her speckled eyes narrowed maliciously.

*Humans...humans...*

There were lots of them. Soldiers, camping soldiers from the east. Which meant axes. Fire and flood always came by one.

She turned her ear to the forest, straining through the perfect quiet, against the occasional howl of the bark-peeling wind, over the thud of snow. But she heard no voices, none at all.

She climbed up onto a north-eastern branch and scurried along to its tip, a limb too weak to have supported anything but her, and looked out into the woods. But she could see nothing, either. No flickering torches, no shadows, no movement. Nothing that didn't belong...

She crouched low and snarled.

*Sneaks. Sneaks!*

Again she returned to the soil, searching for more information. But it was slow, confused - shocked.

Slowly, too slowly, she realised. This wasn't a warning sent from another creature. It was sent by something much simpler.

It was a warning from the plants themselves.

The tree shivered as the cold hand of panic clasped about her throat.

She'd blinded herself. Blinded! This wasn't human at all!

*Not me! Not my tree! No! No!*

The vibration grew closer, rising from a shiver to a shake.

The hand of panic tightened.

She hurried back to the crook of the branches and slipped quickly into the grain, chittering as she rushed down through its veins, down into its roots, just as the sound of cracking ice groaned its way towards her.

What she saw within the earth petrified her. The deeper soil, untouched by the white death, had shifted and crumbled, too quick, much too quick, quicker even than the surface, and already that beneath it had cracked, cracked and shattered - and it was moving right towards her.

Another gnawing wave of cold rushed through her bones as she threw her entire being into the roots, even as the ground beneath began to decompact. She spread them out, broadening her reach across the crack's path, far, far, as far as she could, binding the soil together and holding tightly to anything in reach.

Her efforts didn't daunt it. It snaked forwards, slowly, intently. She watched it through the roots, she listened to it arrive, she felt the stone far below begin to fracture and the soil above it crumble. It pulled at her grip, first like the wind at a leaf, then like a nuthatch on a stubborn grub, then an Arkhamas on a branch, tugging and tugging and tugging until the strain began to ache.

But she didn't release it, no, no, no. She dug in deeper, wider, drawing all her strength, contracting the bark, gritting sharp little teeth tight, so tight.

Roots ripped against the strain, tearing agony through her bones and a feeble hiss from her throat. Wood splintered and creaked, her skin split, sap beaded. But she didn't let go of the riven earth. No, she didn't let go. Even as her strength began to drain and her mind began to spin.

*Not me... Not my...tree...*

She would give everything if she had to. Everything.

Everything.

When the frozen soil finally cracked, the splintered line veered off around her. The break in the rock far below had shifted.

The fracture continued along elsewhere through the forest.

The askafroa collapsed in exhaustion, dropping back into the crook of the great old ash. The ash that remained strong, upright and stoic in the forest, its tangle of roots, clogged in rich, dark soil, stretching far over the edge of the chasm.

She remained there, unmoving, until the morning.

Until the wretched woodpecker came back again.

# To Stalk A Shadow

*Whitewood*

The Arkhamas hit the crimson snow with a light, muffled thump. His giant silver-green eyes stared up through the alder leaves and into the heavily falling snow that thickened the shadows of dusk. His pale skin didn't prickle in the cold.

The slender knife was jerked free from his throat. The blood of the warband was wiped onto a sleeve.

If there was any doubt about the woman's nature, it was lost. She'd moved too fast, too precisely, and had killed too easily something that so closely resembled the children of her own kind.

No, there was no mistaking what kind of monster she was.

The vakah watched her from the shadows, inching slowly closer to the old oak tree. He saw not a hint of remorse in the human's bearing. Once her blades were clean, she moved on without a backward look.

He leaned ruefully in to the nearest branch and whispered briefly to the leaves, his eyes tracking her all the while. He'd arrived too late to save the impulsive band of Arkhamas, but no one else needed to fall. The tree would carry his warning throughout the forest.

But how many would heed it?

Binding his long, green, leaf-sprouting hair behind his head, he stepped back into the shadows, invisible even in his winter hides, and followed the assassin. There was no room for rash action. She was highly trained, even among her own twisted ranks.

And this one had magic, tamed and controlled.

She moved head-on through the storm, purpose in her every unwavering step. The sharp and spinning snowfall thinned visibility to mere paces, and the howl of the wind shrank the range of hearing. But it would have been unwise to assume that it would hinder her. After all, it didn't hinder him.

But he knew already where she was heading. There was little her kind came into the wilds to do but kill, and there was nothing between this forest and the southern coast that would stir her master's political attention. She wasn't merely passing through. Her orders involved these woods. And they were no trial to decipher.

He kept his distance, his feet light, and his eyes fixed closely upon her. He sensed creatures nearby as they shrank silently back out of the way. Good. This was no fight for a raghorn. She was too swift. Too silent. She moved through the forest with barely a sound, seeing everything, hearing everything, and yet seemed to be missed by all.

But that was not magic. That was skill. She, like all of her kind, moved through the world like spectres; they were unseen, unheard, and never remembered, even among humans, hunting whomever their king's orders dictated. Out in the wilds, they moved with less care, yet even so they exhibited the latent skills of the most consummate hunter. The only thing to set them apart was the lack of a bow, and the numb look in their eyes. And their prey out here was not animal, but wildling, for no reason other than misjudgement and dominance.

But, as covert as those gifted with magic among her ranks were, it was difficult to miss its use. Human mages were not usually so clumsy, but mages of this breed had been trained differently; stealth and subterfuge had taken precedence, while magic was merely a tool, a means of securing their deceptions or executions. Their proficiency in physical invisibility was balanced out by loud and stunted casting. Not something other human mages would notice, but his kind certainly would. It was their single redeeming feature. They weren't perfect. Which meant they could be destroyed.

His eyes suddenly tore skyward.

But not by just anyone.

Shrieks ripped through the air, dashed about by the howling wind, and three great raptorial women swept in through the thick snowfall on vast, feathered wings.

The woman turned in a heartbeat. Something flew from her hand.

The battle-shrieks twisted in surprise.

One of the dark forms hit the snow as quickly as it had appeared, and the woman leapt upon it in an instant, vanishing in the cloud kicked up by its struggle.

Frantic squawks rose from the remaining pair as they swept down after her, talons each the full length of an open hand outstretched and grasping. But by the time their powerful wingbeats had fanned away the cloud and falling snow, she'd already pinned the first to the ground, withdrawn the fine blade from its shoulder and slipped it across her feathered throat.

She turned coolly and threw that same blade towards one of the others, and rolled smoothly out of the way of the third. The second met the same fate as the first. Within seconds of the attack beginning, all three winged women lay dead in the blood-stained snow.

She moved on once again without concern. She hadn't even needed a moment to catch her breath.

The vakah suppressed his fury as he followed. He couldn't have saved the harpies without revealing himself. But they hadn't acted foolishly. Not that long ago, this tactic had worked. Her kind had been snooping through the forests for months, and it had been the efforts of harpies and Arkhamas that had so often chased them away.

But something had changed, and recently. Now, they persisted, their ability to feel fear removed by some unnatural sorcery. Now, they could not be dissuaded. Now, they were violent. Nothing could stand in their way. And any that sought to stop them stared directly into the face of their own destruction. Not even humans were exempt.

The only chance was to move unnoticed into striking range, match or exceed their speed and precision, and deliver the killing blow without a moment of hesitation.

Vakehn alone among wildlings had the capacity to stalk and kill these monsters. Few among them possessed the ability to do so without it costing their lives. Fewer still had Rötternas Moder given permission to do so.

He was one of them.

The snowstorm grew stronger. The howls of wolves joined that of the wind. The ephemeral snowflakes struck the skin like needles.

The woman deviated suddenly, striking upwards into a tree and killing an askafroa whose presence he hadn't even noticed.

He steeled and sharpened his focus. Though he privately held no doubt that she was just that attentive.

The forest suddenly opened out, the sprawl of frost-shrouded trees replaced by a myriad of stumps, each topped with a round layer of snow a hand's breadth deep that made the vast, white expanse of the logging site seem that much broader.

She didn't pause at the transition. Neither did he, even as it wrenched at his heart. Because sacrifice was necessary. If they'd tried to protect *everything* from the humans, they would attack and take what they could by force, *wherever* they could, and the wildlings' numbers would fall both by design and consequence. But if a few select areas were set aside for them, they were less likely to trespass, and lives would be saved. They'd already taken to planting their own forests some time ago, an act that had almost been approved of, and those, the forest denizens left alone.

But it still wasn't enough. The natural woods still had to be weighed, judged, and sacrificed. And, lately, it felt as though those sacrifices were mounting.

But he suspected that Rötternas Moder had far more to handle than he could possibly know, and much of it couldn't be done by any hands but hers. Sacrifices simply had to be made, and burdens had to be shared. He didn't envy her the tasks.

He pushed such heavy thoughts from his mind and raised his guard. They were nearing water.

A creek soon ran alongside them, trailing like a black vein through the snow. It was too small to be of use to her, but it was only a matter of time. The creek was a signpost. Its flow was a guide. The woman's path fell in line with it, her feet still as light as the beat of a moth's wings. It didn't take long for another presence to brush the vakah's mind.

His eyes didn't stray, but even in the snowfall he noticed a shimmer of white coalesce on the far bank. A second later, a stallion with a coat purer even than the snow stood beside the running water, watching them as closely as a stalking wildcat.

A bäckahäst. The water spirit wouldn't have heard his warning.

She spotted it herself a moment later, but made no move to attack nor even break her stride. She disregarded it immediately. She seemed to be as resistant to its alluring magic as the enchantments upon the forest itself. She wouldn't have dared to venture in, otherwise.

But the bäckahäst didn't recognise its luck. It gave up its lure and began to follow her instead, nickering sweetly as it drew level across the water.

She loosed a blade towards it. She must have seen its teeth. No true horse had such sharp, fearsome teeth.

The creature fled into the water, vanishing just as the blade passed through it. Here was one, at least, that survived the encounter.

The creek was moving quicker now, and had widened to a stream. She was near her goal. The vakah's adrenaline began to spike. He pressed it into submission.

Sure enough, the sound of faster-flowing water floated from ahead, weaving towards them through the dying gusts of wind.

She abandoned the streamside the moment she heard it, making straight for its source with faultless accuracy.

He adjusted his careful path, silently cursing the dying wind.

Before long, the White River rushed by ahead them.

His eyes dropped to her hands as she approached. With her magic, she could surely break its banks. The näcken's task of keeping the waters flowing had its drawbacks.

And this one seemed ready to amend that.

He tracked the presence of the water spirit while the woman moved towards the waterside, all too aware that there was no way to warn it.

The creature was already waiting when she emerged from the trees, lurking behind his favourite algae-covered rock, watching her closely. He was perfectly hidden. She hadn't spotted him. If she had, he'd be dead.

A sudden splash rose from further along the river. The woman's head snapped towards it.

The vakah moved quietly into position. He had her where he wanted her. She was distracted, at last.

She stepped carefully, slowly along the water towards whatever had disturbed it. But there was nothing there. There never had been. Water moved to näcken's whims, and the näck himself was following her closely. He moved through the water as slick and silent as a fish, with a perfectly honed intent to kill. She'd wandered into his domain without the lure of his violinic voice, and he would

73

take advantage of that.

She spun around so fast that he hadn't managed even to convert his gills when she snatched him out of the water.

His body slammed into the snow, rasping, gasping and spitting, a boy much like an Arkhamas but with green, scaled skin, yellow eyes with frog-like pupils and tattered cloth breeches. The näck thrashed as she pinned it down with her knee and closed her hands about its throat. Gills or not, it was choked to death in moments, and its neck broken for good measure.

She rose as the creature fell still and looked out over the water, the corpse swiftly forgotten. Her expression was cold and void. It hadn't broken once.


The vakah watched her closely from the edge of the trees, noting every detail of her surroundings. He had what he needed.

And so, it seemed, did she.

Her hands rose at last, her fingers contorting into arcane signs. He could feel her magic begin to move.

He crouched quickly, brushed the snow aside, and pressed his palm to the frozen earth. A moment later, he rose and rushed directly for her, his feet as silent as an owl's wings.

A hollow screech ripped through the air.

She spun to stare farther along the water, her spell abandoned, a blade already in her hands, and watched the figure of gnarled twigs and glowing foxfire burst from among the trees and surge straight towards her.

She rushed forwards to meet it.

His reach just missed.

Even as the vakah moved to adjust his own attack, he felt her magic engage again, and orange heat flared through the white forest in an instant, glittering over the water.

The kvistdjur's shriek was deafening. But it was no fool. It threw itself into the river and doused the flames, sending clouds of steam rising from the unruled waters.

But the woman followed after it.

She leapt into the river, seized its horned and thrashing head, planted her boot into its back, and pulled.

Her magic shifted again. It would have been impossible to snap the kvistdjur in half without it.

He spared no moment for pity. This one had heard his warning in the network, and had sacrificed herself to improve his chances. This human would've felt his magic engage at least half as clearly as he had hers. But the kvistdjur had distracted her.

He held his breath. His bare feet pounded the final few steps. His chestnut hands completed their shift from flesh to wood. His fingers stretched into thorny talons. He pulled his elbow back.

She turned and thrust her blade up beneath his sternum, pivoting her body just enough to evade his deadly strike.

For a moment, the world fell still. But even as he disconnectedly felt heat and agony spread through his body, warm blood running down his abdomen, he was already thrusting his other powerful, scything hand into a second attack.

The blade plunged in deeper.

His body shuddered. With the faintest gasp, his efforts sighed away. He collapsed limp against her.

*

The woman stepped back impassively. The forest elf slipped to the snow with a dull and heavy thud. Her eyes returned to the water, this corpse, like all others, forgotten in a moment.

Her hands rose again. Her fingers twisted, her magic swirled in her veins, and her will reached out into the churning waters at her feet.

She didn't notice the grey, bark-skinned woman walk up behind her, nor feel her eyes the colour of painite burning like the flames of ten thousand pyres.

She was dead before her lips could part to scream.


Hlífrún returned to Enar's body. She shook her head as her lips arched in sorrow. The unnatural snow was already trying to bury him.

Silently, she lifted him, and carried him effortlessly into the boundless comfort of the trees.

Laying him gently at the foot of an ancient oak, she knelt and arranged his hands, clasped upon his chest, by his kind's custom. She didn't move back as the roots broke slowly through the snow. She simply watched as they coiled gently around him and drew his body down into the earth. The soil rested lightly upon him.

She didn't go back for the scattered remains of his killer. The wretch would be left for the animals. Its existence wouldn't be entirely wasted.

*Twenty three days.*

*Two powers balanced upon the thinnest ice. Ice cracked by the ghost of a spider's skitter.*
*The world of stone and gold reeled.*

*Day and night roared with the ring of metal, of yelling, of screams; each followed the sun and moon, unbroken by cloud or star. Terror moved behind them like a wind, howling, pushing, ripping; seen, heard and felt by all it reached, deadly with the beat of a gale, destructive with even the glance of a breeze. Hearts stopped or broke in its wake, and new cries joined the cacophony.*

*The sky was cast into orange, burning brightest on every new and hopeless morning, fuelled by hate and vengeance. Trees burned like torches in the distance and the snow itself descended like flames, burning the thick, ashen air laden with the metallic taint of blood.*

*Villages to cities; people fled and gathered, neither sure of safety, trusting only in the distance their feet could carry them from the rage they kept at their backs. But the orange sky, the iron taste, the cries of fallen men and the bellows of the living seemed always to surround them. Even in the depths of the trees.*

# Chapter 11

The heat of the summer air had the most peculiar ability to enhance the scent of a forest. In the far north of Kasire, the rich aroma of damp earth and moss stoked by the latest August deluge rose from the ground like a fog, while sweet, sharp spruce melted down through the air from above. Where they mixed, a heady miasma hung, stirred by the occasional breeze that dragged the scent of wildflowers in its wake. It was impossible to escape, and was trapped itself by the colossal trees.

Those ancients were no less imposing. Growing so tall and so closely packed, only the tops of the spruce had branches and needles, leaving the rest of their towering trunks brown and bare. The sky, too, had vanished in their dominion. Only the vaguest fragments of blue managed to peek through, and shifted like drifting blossom petals.

The sloping forest was left blissfully dark. And there was no blemish of snow here at all.

Bare feet stepped lightly over the uneven ground while twigs crunched beneath her stride, their splintered fragments pressing comfortably against her soles. Hlífrún paused and closed her eyes as another warm breeze whispered across her skin. The chipmunks paused their playful chase across a claw-marked tree, and the boar that had fallen in beside her snuffled at her feet. A soft, contented sigh eased through her lips.

Kasire. Yes, Turunda was beautiful, bathed in the most perfect hues of cascading browns and greens - but Kasire *breathed*. Her mind settled more easily here than anywhere else across her continent. More than once, she'd wished her throne could have stood within these majestic woods.

But not even this landscape was perfect anymore. It, too, had fallen victim to magic - she'd learned long ago that nowhere was safe from the taint of civilisation. But it had at least fared better than Turunda, whose damage she could feel even this far out. And she knew in her blood that it was going to get worse.

Movement caught her attention. A large butterfly, rich scarlet in colour, fluttered between the trees. She watched it weave and change direction, effortlessly making its own path through and against the breeze, flashing its brilliant wings with every undulation. She saw through the disguise immediately.

She kept to herself and walked on, and no sooner had the butterfly disappeared behind a trunk than a stout fellow, clad in a rich scarlet coat, knelt on the other side of it, carefully digging a trowel into the soil with an intent look upon his weasely face. He expertly dug out a few black, dirty truffles as she drew level, then rose and cast her a wide, flourishing bow. "Your Majesty."

"Sharpsnout," she replied with carefully measured courtesy, but she didn't bother to stop. Evidently the forest had impaired her judgement; she must have been too polite, for the vittra fell in step alongside her. "I'm not in the mood for company," she said with a sigh she made only half an attempt to stifle.

"All the more reason to have it."

She cast him a sharp, sideways look as he continued to appraise his truffle with critical sniffs and squeezes. "Forcing yourself into other people's presence when they've politely told you they don't want it might seem cute and quirky to you, but it's a tired practice that's more likely to get your insides sprouting thorns than a declaration of gratitude."

"Perhaps," he said no less coolly, "but I'll bet that passive aggressive comment made you feel a little better."

"No."

"Well, then, perhaps you need to make a few more."

She turned her sneer away and walked on, pretending he wasn't there. It wasn't so easy when she felt his eyes fall back upon her.

"I bet I can make you laugh."

She ignored him.

"What's a tanner's favourite game?"

Still, she ignored him

"Hide and seek."

She couldn't help turning him a flat look. The vittra grinned victoriously as she walked away, though she knew she hadn't smiled at all, and continued to trail along behind her, juggling his truffle. Then he began talking to the boar instead. She listened as he attempted to crack a deal with the creature that would leave them both with half a truffle. After all his sweet-talking, the boar took the whole thing.

"Turunda is at war," she said, for some reason beyond her, as he walked up beside her again.

"Mmmm, yes, I heard. Some petty fued between humans. Something terrible and insignificant, I'd wager."

"The reason doesn't matter," she snapped, albeit half-heartedly. "What *does* is that they're using my forests for fuel and cover, skulking through wherever they please, killing anything they pass and forcing everything else to flee. How am I supposed to fight that along with everything else?"

"I really couldn't tell you."

She folded her arms tightly across her chest. "They're *oblivious* to their impact on the world around them. They take it for granted even as they bleed it dry and believe *they* are the ones that provide for themselves. Nonsense. *Ridiculous*. *Nature* feeds them, *nature* clothes and houses them - the stone for their homes, wood for their fires, flax for their linen, meat and vegetables for their bellies. And it takes *my* effort to keep it alive. To keep *them* alive."

"Your patience is wearing thin, I see. I commend you for not misusing your leverage. I can't say I'd be so noble."

She looked towards him with feigned confusion. She knew he saw through it by the cock of his bushy white eyebrow.

"My cousins plant mykodendrit in food parcels," he explained anyway, she guessed for the sake of her pride. "You could use it to terrorise them. Send them nightmares that soil their beds. But you don't."

"What good would that do us? I only need to discourage them from the purest woods, send them to hunt elsewhere. Suggestion is enough for that. Nightmares on such a scale would seem to them like magic. It would only incite them...and the hunters probably aren't all that responsible for the war anyway..." She kicked at a stick as Sharpsnout stopped to dig his trowel into a particular spot on the ground, and waited without a thought beside him, occupying the boar with affectionate scratches through its wiry fur. It snorted happily, unaware of the distraction, and shook its tufted tail.

"When was the last time you left Turunda?" He asked.

"A couple of weeks ago."

"To wander like this, I mean. Not bridge chasms."

*'Months.'* She stiffened and walked on as he returned. "I've had to

regain my hold."

The vittra sighed dismally, and tossed the truffle he'd just acquired to the boar. "How goes it, then?"

"Voiland, Ithen and Hin'ua have each broken into three or four pieces. I've managed to reconnect them."

"Mhm. And Dolunokh?"

She shook her head. "Sundered completely. Those forests can never be reclaimed." She resented the words as she spoke them.

"What are your intentions?"

"My intentions?"

"Yes, intentions. You know what I mean. What do you plan to do? I ask because I have a family to care for, and while Turunda's wars may not reach me and mine up here, there are families in the south that it certainly will."

That, she could understand. Which made the answer worse. Again her arms folded about herself. "We are answering in kind."

"...Regrettable, but understandable. Where does the mykodendrit fit in? It's freezing, you know. *All* the fungus is suffering."

"*Everything* is suffering, Sharpsnout. As for the mykodendrit, it's growing sluggish. I'm working on it, but warnings and information are slower to spread, too. Harpies and Arkhamas are faster now. They're filling the gap."

His concern was hard to miss. The collected if slightly conniving look he'd worn since appearing faltered quite drastically. "You'd trust the Arkhamas with such an important task? They're still so young a race! As unruly as children, they listen even to *you* only when it suits them--"

"And yet," she spoke over him, "their telepathic abilities are too valuable to shun. They will listen to me."

"They've endeared themselves to you. I'll never understand how."

"Of course they have, and you don't *have* to understand it. Just trust my judgement."

He nodded reluctantly, though he couldn't seem to help shaking his head in disagreement immediately afterwards. She chose not to acknowledge it. "What else? I presume the vakehn are at the forefront?"

"They are." She cocked a woody eyebrow and regarded him with feigned surprise. "You approve, though they're younger even than the *Arkhamas?!*"

"But certainly more reliable, powerful and individually far longer-lived," he noted, raising a finger. "And bow readily to both yourself and Feira. They may not be of sylvan origin, but we as a whole are safer with them than without."

A shadow moved nearby. Though Sharpsnout spun towards it, she didn't need to look up from the fallen needles to know the kvistdjur was there. But she did, and smiled apologetically for disturbing it. The woven creatures were much taller in these woods, and lighter in colour, with heads the shape of moose skulls rather than bear or wolf.

It stared back at them for a long moment, orange firefly eyes glittering in the darkness. Then it flickered, and was gone.

"And safer still with *them*," he added quietly, returning hesitantly to scanning the ground for more truffle spots. "I wouldn't want to be the soldier that upsets one of *them*. They can't be outrun. My brother tried once, and he didn't get very far - about three steps, I think. But," he paused to dig again, "he should've known better than to drink that much brännvin and try to cut down the first dry-looking tree he could find."

"I remember that," Hlífrún mused. "It wasn't the first time he'd done it."

"No, but it *was* the first time he'd mistaken a kvistdjur for the tree he tried to cut down."

She laughed at that, then the vittra looked up towards her and smiled.

"I win."

"Beg your pardon?"

"You laughed." He tossed even this truffle to the boar while she frowned and opened her mouth to protest, and raised his hands in defence, grinning all the while. "I never said you had to laugh at my joke. You'd've looked a damn fool if you did."

"You tricked me."

"Or did you make an assumption because I didn't give you all the details?" She looked down into the hand he removed from his crimson pockets and saw the three enormous truffles he'd had stowed inside. "Just like I didn't show the boar all these. You've mobilised our kin, but you're still taking all the worries onto your own shoulders. Don't assume that you're the only one who can handle all this just because yours is the only power you can see.

Delegate. Trust others in their judgement. And trust that, just because you can't see the efforts others are making, it doesn't mean they're not making them. Turunda's snow isn't all yours to repair. Neither are the chasms all yours to bridge."

She stiffened and glared down at him through suddenly scathing eyes. "You speak of the *Mage*," she hissed.

"He is trying, I'm sure," he replied mildly, waving her irritation away, "though I spoke also of our own kin. But don't forget that *his* world has been impacted by all this as sorely as ours. Why don't you turn a couple of your harpies and Arkhamas out to watch him?"

"I *do*."

"And only have them report back when he *succeeds?*"

She hissed spitefully again, insult steaming in her veins.

"You learn more from failure than success, Your Majesty, take it from me. You should be keeping up with those, too. You're wise enough to know that." He stepped away, quickly stuffing the truffles back into his pocket before the boar could succeed in snatching them from his hand. "Farewell for now, Your Majesty, and good luck. You know where we are, should you need us." With another flourishing bow, the weasel-faced little man turned suddenly back into a scarlet butterfly and danced away through the breeze.

Hlífrún stared after him in outrage - outrage that stemmed, at least in part, from knowing he was right. And also because she suspected the entire encounter had been some manoeuvre to make her look a fool.

She growled and snapped her eyes away toward the distant heights of the trees. The fragments of sunlight glittering between the needles had moved. An hour, perhaps.

She could spare no more time.

With a long and frustrated sigh, she reached out and stroked the boar's wiry muzzle, casting a final glance around at the woods, the bouncing weasels, half-dozing foxes and brown wood owl perched watchfully high up in the branches. The boar pressed its head affectionately into her hand. She managed a meek smile as she bent down and kissed its head before stepping back towards the nearest tree. It shuffled away as she melded into the bark.

The cold as she stepped out again plunged her immediately back into fury.

# Squirrels
### Or *'Death From Above, Below,*
### *And Probably That Bush Over There'*

*Greentop*

There were twelve of them stomping through the woods, their great big boots trampling over everything, breaking sticks and roots like they were eggshells. They moved through anything and everything in their way like it didn't matter to no one at all. They *were* being careful, though, in their own way: their eyes were flicking about, and they were being *kind of* quiet when they walked - quiet for a human, anyways. But they were only looking out for their own kind. Anything else could spot them from a mile off - and they wouldn't spot those 'anything else' even if they were standing right in front of them and poking them in the eye.

*That probably ain't true - be fun to try, though!*

But it wasn't *quite* worth putting to the test. Things were too serious for those kinds of games right now.

The Arkhamas continued to stalk through the trees, moving like three-foot tall squirrels, leaping silently from branch to branch. They'd learned the trick ages ago. Not *from* squirrels, though. And even if those tawny-skinned fellas did look up, he and his warband had covered their scraggly hair with chalk dust - and all the twigs and leaves and bird nests tied into it and all. And their skin was already plenty light enough, especially when they wore white hides or the white shirts they'd pinched from washing lines.

It was kind of a shame though, really. Nug liked covering himself in mud and leaves. It was half the fun of a hunt. But if he did that now, he'd stick out like a thumb that had been stung by seven bees, and a particularly angry wasp. And the mud probably wouldn't spread very well, either.

Still, they all felt naked without it, and not the good kind. But it was what it was and it would have to do. It had worked so far, at any rate.

His oversized, silver-green eyes scanned about the forest as he went. It was still way too open. There weren't enough trees to jump down from. There was a good ambush spot further in - but they had to herd the soldiers there first.

*Probably not* all *of 'em, though...*

His curious gaze fell back to the humans. Their half-plate armour didn't do much to make them less obvious. The metal reflected the snow all right, but the leather was too colourful. It would probably have been just fine if the forest was still normal, but now they looked as bright as daffodils. But not yellow. Actually, it probably wouldn't have made much difference if they *were* yellow.

The five other members of his warband were deciding the same.

His decision went out.

*'The third one.'*

*'Yeah, the third one.'*

*'From the back, yeah?'*

*'You're so annoying.'*

He cackled silently to himself and hung back while the others advanced, lifted his hands to his lips and gave a sharp whistle. A starling, roughly - close enough that the humans wouldn't notice anything wrong with it - and moved on to join the rest as a smooth, matching noise replied from high above. The harpies were informed. And they already knew they were counting from the back. It'd been agreed before the stalk. Zeb was just a tosspot.

The humans didn't react to any of it, mind. Of course they didn't. How could *birds* be a threat?

The path the invaders had cut had widened briefly, and Nug took up his position in the slippery boughs of an oak. The others, except one, were scattered through the rest of the trees, ringing the soldiers from above. All eyes were on the third (from the back), and the snow-covered-twig-covered ditch at the edge under a hornbeam.

Nug stifled a snicker as the soldier moved towards it and vanished in a poof of snow. They knew they'd get him there. That one always veered to the left whenever his path got wider. Maybe he had a short leg. Either way, he was a freebie. No trouble at all.

A convenient magpie call went up, covering the sound of the tumbling sticks and frightening the rest of the jittery soldiers so they looked away, and the lass hiding in the hornbeam dropped from the branches and straight into the ditch on top of him. She was so fast he didn't even get the chance to scream in surprise.

She scrambled back out in seconds, and another of the warband made a distraction up ahead to draw the soldiers on while she cleaned the blood off herself in the snow. They took the bait almost too easily. The lass scurried back up into the tree while they moved forwards, totally oblivious to their soldier-friend's 'accident', and the Arkhamas duly followed.

The trees closed back in. Before long there was another opening up ahead, a gap in the leaves. It was better suited to the harpies than them.

*'They can do this one. The feller at the back.'*

It was a risk, but they knew all too well how good the harpies were at killing. They were freakishly fast and quiet. And the sun was ahead of them, which meant shadows weren't a problem neither.

A chaffinch that wasn't a chaffinch sounded from the trees nearby, then a bullfinch chirped the position.

Another not-a-chaffinch called back from above, and as soon as the soldiers moved into the pocket of cold light, a giant half-eagle-half-woman shot in through the trees as fast as an arrow, grabbed the soldier, punctured his throat with a right fearsome talon, and dragged him back up into the air and out of sight.

Nug stared after it with begrudging awe. She really didn't make a noise. Not even the leaves rustled with the beat of her humongous wings.

His skin prickled. Thank the Lady they weren't enemies right now.

He heard the body thump heavily into the snow a short ways back, but the soldiers hadn't noticed the abduction. They and the warband continued moving forwards.


There weren't any more opportunities for a while. The forest was thick with loads of trees to jump down from, and lots of openings for the harpies too, but the damned humans kept switching their path and bypassed any trap they'd laid. Then a kvistdjur starting singing somewhere close by and frightened them all enough to send them running off in some random direction. One of them even bumped into one of the trees and almost knocked Ren out of it. She managed to keep herself in by grabbing hold of the trunk, but it was way too close.

Chased them down, though - and of course they realised they'd lost two of them ages ago by that point - and managed to regain some control, but it'd taken so long that the soldiers could've found whoever they were looking for by then and started a dirty great brawl in the middle of their woods.

They didn't, though, but at least two more of those soldiers should've been taken down by the time the next chance finally showed itself.

But they made do. They had no choice, especially since the next target wasn't of their picking. The seventh fella in the group, near the front, wandered too close to the trap.

It was another ditch - it had been more varied than that, but they'd bypassed the more exciting ones - and while another Arkhamas managed to get into position quickly enough to quiet the man's shout and kill the bugger, the others were looking their way. It was only the quick efforts of the harpies that saved their skins, mimicking in their weird, hollow voices some nonsense they'd heard the Doanan soldiers shout at some time in the past. Nug had no idea what it was, and didn't really care. Aside from the funny tongue clicking, it didn't really sound all that fun to repeat. Mostly because they'd already tried to work out how to make the noise but it just came out like clucking. And the harpies could only do it because they were cheats.

Whatever the case, they saved them, and a third soldier was eliminated.

But they were getting jumpy now, and noticed he was missing. They found the body way too quickly.

That wrote off the rest of the ditches. They'd be more careful, and were already moving closer together. The warband knew they wouldn't get away with much more.

There was nothing for it but to hang back for a while.


Nug almost slipped in the frozen bird-splat and fell off his branch at the next event. A shout went up among the nine jittery soldiers, and the Arkhamas stilled in panic. The harpies weren't in sight, the icy leaves were too thick, and they were each sure themselves that they hadn't been seen.

Of course when a tell-tale roar went out, it was pretty clear what was responsible.

The raghorn burst out of the blue shadows and set upon the soldiers like a hawk on a rabbit. Except it used its antlers rather than any talons, so maybe that wasn't the best comparison. Either way, the fella was skewered in moments.

Even the Arkhamas stared in shock while the soldier was shaken off, his red blood spattering the snow, and watched as the rest of his friends shed their own terror and charged for it with their swords. They always did that. Nug had always thought they'd get smarter in a group, but they only got dumber. So another one was impaled.

But the rest weren't so dazed by the second kill, and made to stab it right quick.

Nug sent out the order.

As one, the Arkhamas began firing their slingshots through the branches. They didn't have many stones, but they were all a good shot, so it didn't take long for the soldiers' attention to turn to the trees, and since these sneaky types didn't have much to protect their eyes, a few well-placed stones either side of the nose was generally enough to upset them, and enough, it seemed, for them to forget about their own arrows, too. Really, though, they should've seen the stones coming.

Nug cackled to himself as he lined up another shot right in the eye of a particularly steel-clad fella. It hit with a satisfying thunk. He hadn't seen that one coming, either.

The raghorn didn't flee in a rush, and managed to injure a few more of them before finally withdrawing. They were useful creatures, guards that prowled through the forests, and almost kind of friendly when you gave them fresh rabbits. No Arkhamas wanted to see them killed. They let them ride them, too - or, they were quick to give up on their objections, at any rate, and didn't buck *too* often.

The soldiers still hadn't spotted them, but it wasn't worth giving them the chance. As soon as the raghorn was out of sight, one of the lads tugged free the walnut shell that was tied around his neck, shook it, then slingshotted it down into the chaos. The shell broke against one fella's head, and two very angry wasps popped out. The rest of them ran off in a panic while the unfortunate stingee trailed after them, yelping and certainly breaking their cover.

The warband had a good laugh at that before they followed along.

*'Seven left.'* One of the others provided. *'We can take 'em, easy.'*
*'It ain't far.'*
*'Let the turk--'* Nug rolled his eyes. *'Let the* harpies *know.'*

A cuckoo's song sprung up close by, and another answered from above.

The Arkhamas' good humour vanished like a mosquito.

They moved on, their focus sharp. There was no time to slip on bird-splat now.

The forest changed as they neared the old oak grove; the trees became thicker, broader, and the ground was lumpier. The soldiers didn't seem to notice the change, but they certainly got frustrated with tripping over. They were panicking - and swearing, probably. It was a weird language, but people didn't tend to say words so viciously to themselves unless they were curses.

But then another sound rose up that silenced everyone, and put curses into the Arkhamas' mouths instead.

The sound of a violin in the middle of the forest, a forest filled with snow, in wartime - it was enough to upset anyone, really. But the soldiers seemed to know what it meant. They adjusted their path right away.

*'Damned näcken!'*
*'They're going the wrong way!'*

Nug broke his position and rushed on ahead. A couple of trees rustled as he ran through them, but the soldiers didn't seem to notice it. It didn't really matter now, anyway, since they were already jumping at shadows.

He scrambled down to the snow when he got ahead of them, and scurried a little way into the trees - just enough that he was hidden. Then he began to growl. He snarled and grunted like a hungry pig, some kind of mad pig with meat on its mind. That was the idea, anyway. He made as much noise as he could, stomping the ground, kicking wood, snarling, grumbling, salivating, and moving slowly closer to the soldiers. They stared into the shadows with terror on their faces. Nug didn't see it, though - he was too absorbed in his part. So absorbed that he'd lost control a little bit and dribbled on himself.

When he heard them dash off, half-shouting to one another, probably to hurry up, he grinned victoriously, wiped his mouth and chest, and scurried back up into the trees to join the others. They tracked the soldiers back onto the path, his comrades correcting them with a few grunts and growls of their own until they were well on their way, the *right* way.

The soldiers, good boys that they were, were running now, and making up for the warband's lost time. They weren't the only meddling buggers in the woods that needed clearing out, and it was getting close to supper time.

At that thought, Nug's attention was even quicker to steel.

*'We're here.'*

The Arkhamas broke away.

Three sped up. Three fell back. All took positions.

The soldiers slowed to a stop in the middle of the gnarled old grove and fell to their knees in the shadows of the oaks, exhausted, panting like dogs, their grips lazy around their swords. They'd not heard anything in a while. They probably quite fancied a rest.

Then they should've stayed at home.

Deep, dull thuds came from somewhere close to the east. The soldiers' eyes dashed towards it, brightening nervously.

It came again to the south-west, and they spun towards that, too. Then again further west.

They rose heavily back to their feet, huddling together like frightened sheep, and looked hopefully towards the north. They started towards it, until sharp trills rose up from that direction, too.

Then the thumping came again.

The Arkhamas thudded their feet against the tree trunks in powerful bouts, no two sounding at the same time, all around the soldiers. Then came the scratch of quills - the harpies were in position.

Nug quickly pulled the walnut free from around his neck and cracked it against the tree, then dripped the awful-smelling liquid inside over the tip of his wooden spear. He was as careful as he could be while the adrenaline ran through his blood. It wouldn't do to get the poison *all* over his hands.

The last voice of the warband sounded in his head as he cleaned his hands off in the snow. He leaned around, took a deep breath, and aimed his voice towards the shaking soldiers.

"*Boomf!*"

Their eyes tore his way just as he darted back behind the tree. It was the perfect sound: too strange to be natural, too weird to be careless, but too loud to be an accident. It was the perfect thing to confuse them.

The harpies answered his attack signal immediately.

Nug squinted as he watched three huge shadows descend over the sun - shadows that once would've called for a defensive attack of their own. If the soldiers weren't scared, they really should've been.

Arrows were loosed from thwanging strings, but they were useless, either missing and firing into the blaze that glared down behind them, bouncing off of their massive wings, or blown back by great powerful flaps. No, stones weren't as 'streamlined', if you wanted to get technical, but they were heavier and harder to knock off-course. But he wasn't about to tell the soldiers that.

Two giant eagles appeared, too - the harpies' young, still more bird than bird-people, but Nug guessed they'd been brought along for training. Harpies didn't really play or prank like Arkhamas did, so they had to learn somehow. But they were much faster than their parents, and made a brilliant job of confusing the scene. It was usually chaos, but the Arkhamas were free to ignore them this time. Today, anything with feathers was not a target.

He gripped his spear tightly. His hands were shaking with adrenaline. He watched the fight begin, his giant eyes sharp, his mouth exploding into a grin. This was the very best bit.

The moment the first talons met flesh, Nug gave the order.

The soldiers spun in shock as the six child-like attackers shot out from the trees with a great war cry, their viciously sharp wooden spears held high, some coated in worryingly bright orange fluid, others bare but absolutely promising splintery agony.

Nug relished that stunned and desperate confusion. Even as their eyes darkened and their blades turned towards them, it was a hilarious sight. Because then their eyes widened and looked down at their feet as the ground fell away from them, and their dark skin paled, kind of, when they felt the rush of nausea in their stomachs and the pinch of claws in their shoulders.

Nug had felt that fright before. But now he couldn't help but grin at the terror of his new enemies.

He and his comrades set upon them with glee, and when the harpies let go of a few a little too soon, they were quick to run over and make sure the job was finished when they hit the ground.

There would be no mercy.

These were *their* woods, their *homes* these soldiers were trampling and destroying, even turning them into their own battlegrounds! They *had* to defend it. After all, he didn't go into *their* homes and drag his fights along with him, knocking over walls or scratching up their furniture! And if he did, just what would humans have done to him that would've been so different from this? If they didn't have swords, they'd have bludgeoned them all to death with a rolling pin instead. Because they were different, and humans were afraid of that.

Well, *they* were all afraid, too.

Nug dashed over to another soldier that fell out of the sky, but he was already dead. His head almost definitely shouldn't have been at that angle.

Another dropped beside him, but though this one groaned, the harpy that had let go of him swooped back in before Nug could turn and tore him to pieces with her beak.

Nug shied away, pulling a face. That, fortunately, *hadn't* happened to him, but it had been close a few times, and he didn't much like to see it.

But when he turned to charge back in to the fight, he found all of the soldiers lying still in the red snow, mostly in one piece.

It was over - and this time, none of his warband had died!

His grin spread again and hot relief made his bones start shaking. But he ran anyway, tripping a couple of times, and joined them as they jumped and cheered in victory, pulling faces and kicking snow over their slain enemies.

The harpies alighted nearby, lifting their feet from the freezing snow in disgust, and watched them with their usual annoying, yellow disapproval.

"Do not let your guard down," one of them scolded in their strange sort of way, her beak parted while her hollow voice rattled somewhere in her throat, but Nug just beamed, since he knew it would annoy them.

"Awh, *relax!*" He cackled when those poisonous eyes narrowed. "We won!"

"This time."

"And we'll win all rest, innit!" Ren declared, her cheerful face splattered with blood. Nug realised his own was the same. He could see it if he crossed his eyes.

But the harpy hissed at them humourlessly. "You are too brash!"

"But," another squawked, "your confidence in victory *is* to be admired."

Then, without another word, the three jumped up into the air and propelled themselves away with a powerful flap of their wings. Quite rudely, really.

Nug grumbled as snow hit him in the face.

"Do you reckon they can actually *say* 'goodbye'?" Another said as they watched them and their young vanish over the trees.

His lips pursed in thought. "They might still have to learn it. If we shout it after 'em, it's bound to help."

And so they did, right at the top of their lungs, then dashed, cackling, back into the woods.

# Hope

*Whitewood*

Was it snow, she pondered? Or was it sea? Was it frost-glow or cloud-glare? There were no stars to mark the difference on the horizon that night. Snow had eaten everything. And whichever it was, a harpy was made for neither.

A keen whistle drifted through the frozen air. Her sharp, yellow eyes turned out to the kestrel hanging a quarter mile out above the white meadow, and she answered in kind. She had already eaten her fill. She did not need more.

The kestrel stooped into the silver grass and rose again with the vole clutched in his talons.

The harpy nestled deeper into the forking alder at the southernmost edge of the woods. Fluffing bronze feathers against the penetrating cold, her stare turned back to the small camp far below. The amber glow of the fire was appealing. It promised an end to the cold, and did not stir even in the frigid gusts that rocked the heights of her perch. The stone bank shielded it from the wind of the snow-sea.

But the life of the flame was not her concern. Her duty that night was to watch and report.

A small clutch of figures moved below with the rising smell of ruined meat. Humans. But only one was of consequence - one with pale skin and black hair, wrapped in a dark cloak, standing restless beside the flames while his companions ate. The Mage. It was he she fixed her hawk-like gaze to. And he that hatched something called 'hope' inside her.

It was a strange feeling. A kind of anticipation, but one without reason. She had never experienced it before - there had never been need of it. Everything had always been as it should have been; good or bad, everything happened by design. But where the biting cold had come in every year before, her flock had known of it. They had felt it coming. Heard it. Seen it. This, they had not seen. Their prey had not seen it. And now hunting was difficult, and the recent change of territory and alliance made it harder still.

But that was why she hoped. And why Rötternas Moder hoped.

Another waft of hot rabbit reached her nostrils, and the word 'snow' was spoken below. Her attention sharpened.

She heard the doubts that followed. She heard the Mage refute them. He extended his hand, and another reluctantly put something in it. Something small and black and glinting, a puny thing of metal. But this puny thing was the key. The Mage had used it often to complete his magics - but could something so small possibly fix something so great?

It had to. Nothing else could, or it would have by now.

She watched closer.

Far below, the Mage stepped back from the fire. The light did not reach him so easily, but the metal thing, shaped like a straight-edged beak, caught the glow. It glittered golden. The few others with him stood back and watched. Their faces were uneasy.

All fell still. She could hear their heartbeats. She felt her own. She fluffed her feathers absently against the teasing wind.

The metal thing began to float between his hands. No one stirred, but their hearts beat faster. That of the Mage most of all.

For some time, nothing changed. Only the wind had no care for the matter. The wind stopped for nothing. That was how it should be, and that unchanging fact also gave her hope.

Then the others began to fidget. They turned their heads, they looked around, ahead, behind, beside them. She, too, turned her keen eyes across the snow. Nothing as yet had changed.

Minutes passed. Gusts shook. A wolf pack howled in the distance.

Finally, the Mage grunted. A meek sound, like that of a mouse. The smallest of his companions stepped towards him, but he did not react. Even from the height of the tree, she could see his eyes were closed tight. Even among the endless snow, she could see the sweat on his brow. Even as he stood motionless, she could see his strength leave him.

Then he staggered and faltered, and the smallest reached out to catch him. She heard a profound curse as he collapsed. It had been muttered, and it meant nothing to her, but its intent was clear.

This was not the first time he had failed. Nor the first time one of her kind had witnessed it.

Her feathers flattened in disappointment, and her hope faded with the rest.

What had gone wrong? It was beyond her wisdom to guess. Perhaps even beyond that of Rötternas Moder. Her magic was different, after all.

Perhaps it was him. Perhaps it was his method. But she could not see that he had done anything at all, and failed to understand how the puny, floating trinket could help in the first place. But she had rarely seen magic so close, and made no attempt to apply what little she knew to an explanation. It was not her task to do so. Only to watch and report.

Rötternas Moder would appreciate the news. It may anger her, but she would be pleased to know that the Mage was trying. It would calm her heart, whether she wished his help or not.

But for the moment, she was full. The rabbit filled her belly. She would report in the morning. Perhaps another of her kin would witness the next attempt. Perhaps it would be herself. And perhaps it would be that attempt which would finally succeed.

She settled and fluffed again, watching his companions assist him to the fire side and the small one tuck the metal thing away in the bags borne by their tusked beasts.

His head sank into his hands. No one spoke for a long while.

Another frigid gust shook through the branches.

# The Girl In The Crystal Tree

*Ziili*

One day, in a white and twinkling forest, there was a beautiful tree encased in crystal. It stood taller than the rest, glinting in the sun like diamonds, and no bird dared land within its ancient branches for fear of causing it harm. It was a majesty among trees, a true wonder to behold.

The lowly boy couldn't help but visit it every day. Straying from his chores, he would peek out from the river with his frog-like eyes, wide in awe and hope, and marvel at its grandeur.

But it was not, in all truth, the tree he came to see.

He waited that morning as he always did, in the river at the foot of the tree, his breath short and bated, until the lofty leaves began to tinkle and her face finally appeared. Fair and pale, it peeked timidly from between the glittering leaves, framed by long, draping hair of the softest spider silk, decorated beautifully with glinting lichen and interrupted only by the slender, twig-like tips of her ears. Her nose was dainty, her lips were fine, and her big, piercing, speckled eyes the colour of floating pondweed made his stomach flutter as they fell upon him.

Then, the girl's fine lips parted, her perfectly pointed teeth were bared, and her voice whispered out towards him in a delicate, venomous hiss.

He smiled foolishly before submerging his own slovenly maw beneath the water that flowed black against the tree's glory. There, he opened his mouth, and sang. His voice the sound of bowing strings danced like currents through the water, weaving together before breaking the surface, entwined into an ethereal melody so beautiful that it stilled even the hunt of bears, so fragile, wistful and haunting.

She watched him closely through his serenade, her mysterious eyes sharp and narrow, and slunk slowly through the tree towards him, loosing fine showers of diamonds as she went. The sprawling crystal bough that reached lowest over his river barely moved as she climbed along to its tip, and tinkled like glass as she lay herself down upon it.

He sang more hopefully.

The sudden, graceful swipe of her petite, clawed hand just missed the top of his head.

The boy's song ceased as she swiped again with another hiss, and he cast her another foolish smile before diving back beneath the water and swimming away.

The girl in the ash tree watched him vanish into the quietly flowing river, staring after him until he was certainly gone.

Her lips twitched up into the slightest smile as she disappeared back among her branches.

* * *

The next morning, in the white and twinkling forest, the soft, chiming song of tousled diamond leaves stirred the fine fall of snow into a merry dance. Glowing in the shine of a hidden sun, it twirled and looped through the air like flakes of pure silver, settling silently upon branches and stones and softening the hardest edges.

Once again the boy arrived quietly at the foot of the proud, crystal tree, where the black river bent and skirted the reach of its ancient roots, and waited with bated breath until its tinkling leaves announced her arrival and the girl's fair face finally appeared.

Her skin was even paler in the fall of the snow, her piercing eyes more vibrant, and the gentle breeze that rustled leaves and rippled the surface of his water dishevelled her silken hair. Her eyes found him, and his stomach fluttered.

The tinkling of the leaves softened her wonderful warning hiss.

Heedlessly, with his slovenly maw beneath the black water, his own voice moved, entwining and rising again in his hopeful serenade.

Her fine, slight body moved silently through the tree, watching him very closely, and lay down at the end of the branch.

His song deepened. This time, he dared to swim closer.

Again her hissing swipe just missed the top of his head.

He cast her another foolish grin, but after dodging the second graceful swipe, he rose up, dropped something onto the bank from his green, webbed hands, then dove backwards and vanished beneath the water.

The girl in the ash tree watched him vanish into the quietly flowing river, staring after him until he was certainly gone.

Her eyes dropped to the three stones he'd left on the ground.

She tied her legs about the end of the branch, dropped her slender body down and snatched the rocks from the snow, three smooth, round pebbles that had been chipped into the shape of leaves.

Her lips twitched up into the slightest smile as she disappeared with them back among her branches.

* * *

The next morning, in the white and twinkling forest, the snow fell heavily, with no music to stir it so merrily nor sunlight to make it glint. The sky was dark, the clouds thick, and the glitter of the trees dulled in the thick stillness. Only the towering crystal tree jostled, its leaves ringing in agitation, and cast sparse lights like silver fireflies through the forest.

The boy knew something wasn't right even before he arrived at the foot of the tree, at the bend in the river, in the shelter from the snow, and as he swam closer he felt the tremors through his water, shaken by heavy stomps and booming bellows.

He poked his head through the surface and looked along towards the tree. His stomach fluttered in rage.

Six steel-skinned beasts had surrounded it; three at the bank with sharpened arrows pointing up and through the leaves, and three with swords that reached for branches and jammed their steel boots into the trunk for hold. And, far above them, the pale-skinned, silken-haired, piercing-eyed girl scrambled nimbly through the branches, avoiding the flying arrows and swiping with perfect ferocity at the reaching, grasping hands.

The boy swam on, a fire in his belly like a salamander's fury, and burst from the river behind the steel-skinned monsters without a thought for safety, a spray of water twinkling like glass behind him.

While one of the bladed beasts suddenly collapsed from the tree and spasmed uncontrollably in the snow, the boy snared one of the arrowed, snapped the shaft and slashed the head of it across the beast's throat.

While another of the bladed screamed and clawed at the blood pouring from beneath his helmet, another of the arrowed was mauled, and his nose cleanly bitten off.

While the last of the bladed dropped from the lowest branches and landed still, staring in silence as the whites of his eyes turned red, the last of the arrowed was kicked in the head and toppled backwards, dragged heavily into the river.

The boy breathed at last as water flooded back over his gills, and the final steel-skinned monster drifted, dazed and drowning, down along the currents. His body shook like a summer leaf, his heart thudded like a bäckahäst's hooves, and his aching, seizing muscles were slow to loosen.

But his trials were forgotten and his stomach fluttered again when he found the girl looking down at him from the crystal branches. He smiled foolishly, even when she hissed, but she seemed too tired to scurry forwards to attack him. And he was too exhausted to sing.

But that didn't matter. She was safe.

So he turned and slowly swam away to recuperate in his pool. He would come back to sing later, and she would swipe at him, if she was feeling any better.

The girl in the ash tree watched him vanish into the quietly flowing river, staring after him until he was certainly gone.

Then she began to shake. Her twiggy arms wrapped around herself as she watched the snow disintegrate the moment it touched his calm water, the river that wound through the forest like a dauntless guardian, a life-bringer, a black smudge of hope in a world of dead and biting white, where sky and land merged indistinctly along the distant horizon.

She and her frosted tree should have died. Such violent curses weren't quick enough to act, not against six beasts. They were too many, and too strong.

...But the boy had saved her. And had almost suffocated doing it.

Her lips twitched up into the slightest smile, and she hugged herself tighter. She didn't disappear back among her branches.

* * *

The girl remained on the rivermost branch that night, staring absently into the black water, studded with stars as though the clear night's sky had fallen and been laid out like a gift before her. Her fine lips pouted as she fiddled with the leaf-shaped stones. The boy hadn't come back yet. She'd wanted to thank him.

She closed her eyes and listened intently to the song that seemed to rise from beneath her. The boy was nowhere near, yet it felt as though he sang for her. It was the same ethereal melody, the melody that stilled even the hunt of bears, fragile, wistful and haunting. The melody that softened her thoughts like the brush of the warm summer sun, that quieted her heart like the rustle of wind through her leaves, that lowered her guard so much that it frightened her, and she lashed out though she knew there was nothing in it but love. And that frightened her, too.

She sighed, entranced and resentful, lost in the tune, and barely cast a glance towards the light of war-fire that rose in the distance.

The lowly boy watched the stars from deep below the water as he sang his heartsick song. It was a beautiful night, the cloud shattered as though the stars had forced their way through to rejoice in the girl's safety. As so they should. What other reason was there to shine so brightly?

But as his eyes drew back in the direction of the magnificent tree, the tree he imagined would reflect the starlight as perfectly as though it had captured it itself, a glowing smudge of colour had erased the night beyond. And, as he watched it, the orange smudge seemed to grow.

A phantom urgency drove him forwards from his cascading pools, his song unceasing as he frowned and swam. He'd quite forgotten he was singing at all, but when he noticed, he found that he didn't dare stop lest the ominous shadow that had begun to follow creep up over him.

Even from beneath the water, the sky burned orange and black, and the heat that rippled over the surface distorted the picture into even taller flames.

The ominous shadow crashed over him like rapids long before his song fell silent.

Panic gripped him for the second time that day, pushing him on through the heat towards the river bend. He saw the crystal tree through the water, its silver trunk as black as coal, its diamond leaves aflame, and all thought burned away with the towering ancient's pride.

He began to spin frantically, whipping the water into turmoil and raising it higher and higher, as high as the blazing branches, and sent the waterspout crashing down upon it. But beneath the great cloud of steam, the inferno continued to burn.

The boy tried again, and again, but the flames wouldn't die. Branches fell, embers rose, soot-blackened snow burst up on impact into heavy puffs, and the fire continued its malicious dance, catching on tree after tree, spreading deeper through the forest.

The boy, exhausted but relentless, tried for the ninth time, and after that ninth sizzling cloud of steam, a small, pale shape dropped heavily from the tree.

He burst from the water without thought of heat or breath, and reached for the girl's delicate form. Her pale skin was charred and smoking, her draping, silken hair was gone, and she neither hissed nor swiped nor narrowed her piercing eyes. Even as he lifted her from the snow, her skin searing and steaming his own, she didn't move nor make a sound.

The heat was stifling so close to the tree, and he'd forgotten again to alter his gills. He couldn't breathe. He had to get back to the water.

But he couldn't bring her with him. She would drown, and taking her too far from the roots of her tree would doom both her and it. There would be no regrowth. No flourishing. No hissing. No love.

But if he suffocated, and others of her forest kin weren't close by, who would be there to save her?

As his final breath threatened to expire, he was forced to make the choice.

He held her close and hurried back towards the water. Water nourished her tree's roots. Perhaps it could help her after all.

The boy did not notice the shadow that appeared behind him on silent feet, nor did he ever learn that his neck was snapped, that the fire spread, nor that the girl he'd so dearly loved had died in relief the moment he'd taken her into his arms.

# First Rule Of The Hunt

*Sotwolds*

The mournful horn blared deafeningly again, leading yet another volley of whistling arrows through the trees. Dogs barked and howled, and the sound of human voices urging faster the thud of hooves rose from somewhere in the tangle behind them.

The raghorn sprinted through the forest. Panic had sharpened her focus. Her eyes flicked through the golden light of the early morning for anything that could guide her to safety. But there was little to see or smell that would help. She could only run on and find firmer ground that would leave smaller tracks.

She breezed over logs, launched onto rocks, bounded over clearings and adjusted her course at random; her paws gripped down into the snow and sharpened her turns, her breaths were short and efficient, and her great, black, crescent-moon antlers were held low, angled just enough to cut a little quicker through the air.

The clamour began to fall further away, but she didn't dare slow down. They wouldn't be so easily lost. The arrival of the unnatural snow hadn't stopped this hunt - if anything, it seemed more fervent. And there were more of them than usual.

Barking burst suddenly from the trees behind her, sending another blinding fire through her blood. She raised a paw even as she sprinted and loosed a quick and powerful swipe. The hound yelped and thumped into a tree. She didn't waste time looking back.

The humans were nearing already. She could hear them. They'd followed the barks.

She veered around and branched away, dashing quickly through the trees, tracking their mounts' hoofbeats, keeping their position in the very centre of her focus. Then she burst through the trees, just like the hound.

She'd found them.

The raghorn leapt at the rearmost hunter from behind. A dog barked even before she struck, but they were too slow to react. The horse screamed in fright as her antlers gored its liveried rider.

The alarm went up, and the other hunters spun in their saddles, nocking arrows and shouting. But their quarry had already fled, bounding away back through the forest.

Their tactics had changed. They'd learned too quickly. One of the hounds had been called back to keep watch. She'd taken down three hunters with these looping attacks already, thinning their count to nine, and she knew she wouldn't manage it again.

Barking closed in from the east. The rest of the dogs were back on her trail. They would never stop.

She shifted her winding route just as another volley of arrows fired through the trees, thunking into wood and bouncing off stone behind her. A few whistled past her head; just one hit her bloodied antler. She spared it no notice.

She ran on until a rustle behind a rocky outcrop snapped her attention to the right, and lowered her head as a shadow broke away.

The hound plunged from the rocks onto her antlers with a frightened yelp. It made no other sound when she tossed it to the snow.

The doleful horn rose up again from beyond the outcrop, and she bolted in the opposite direction. It was only the snort of irritated horses that gave her warning enough to dodge the arrows that fired towards her as she charged blindly into a clearing and the rest of the waiting hunting party.

A steamy puff burst from her muzzle as she spun around frantically, stirring up the snow, her grip lost in her surprise. She managed to dash back into the trees without an arrow's graze.

Her blood burned with adrenaline.

They'd tricked her.

She couldn't fall into a trap like that again.

Her eyes searched desperately. A bare tree split down the middle a short bound to the left gave her a flood of hope.

She veered towards it and followed the stream, then broke away at a tall, slender stone and branched off to the left. The morning light dimmed; the trees grew thicker, and the land rose into a sheer slope, its face studded with narrow rock ledges barely the width of her own paws.

She leapt upon it immediately.

Her claws dug into stone and ice for purchase and she climbed the cliff at speed, tilting her head and antlers away from the catching rock. She was lithe and limber enough to manage it; the dogs couldn't follow far, and the horses would be stuck at the bottom. She would get to the top, follow the dry riverbed, and she would be safe at last.

She followed the cliff up and above the tops of the trees until bright sunlight and blinding snow coated every foothold. She looked along the rockface, but above and to either side, every ledge was hidden beneath a smooth blanket of freezing gold. And the top was still too far to jump.

The ledge her claws had pierced into began to crumble beneath her feet. If she tried to go on, claws or not, she would lose her footing and fall. There was no way up, and no way along.

Her eyes turned back towards the silvered treetops. There was only down.

She saw no choice.

She descended just as quickly as she'd climbed until she was back among the leaves, then made her way along the cliff. The height she'd climbed would still have lost them, she just had to make sure she didn't catch their notice again. Then she'd be free.

The sheer face began to decline as she moved further along, making for another outcrop that jutted out into the forest. She could make the jump easily, and then be half way between the forest floor and the top of the cliff. They wouldn't find her there.

A low growling quickly sank that hope.

Another hound stood, hackles raised, at the top of the jutting outcrop. A second appeared behind it.

She snorted in growing desperation.

The first hound lunged.

Her claws lashed out swiftly. The strike sent it tumbling down the slope and out of sight. A plaintive wail soon rose up from the forest floor.

The second hound barked and growled savagely, but it didn't attempt the jump.

Her only chance now was to leap over it.

There was no time to second-guess. Her powerful feline legs bent, her strength gathered, and she launched herself off from the narrow ledge. The dog barked furiously, snapping at the air and spreading its paws to jump up and catch her as she flew, but changed its mind in the final moment.

It made no difference. She landed behind it and kicked out her back feet, thrusting it off and on down the escarpment. The other dog was still wailing. The second didn't join it.

She ran on, heart hammering, lungs burning, legs aching despite the invigoration of hope. But she knew she couldn't run forever. They would never stop. And it wasn't her alone the humans sought. Once they bested her, they would seek another raghorn. She had to break their confidence, once and for all.

She heard hunters and horses up ahead, and once again ran straight into them. They were closer than she'd realised. She stumbled in the snow as she turned away, arrows already loosed and flying, but this time something hit her leg as she fired back off into the woods.

She roared in fury, but didn't turn antler or claw upon them. Instead, she focused.

Onwards she ran, shaking her gory crown in rage, blood dripping in the snow behind her as she limped, aware all the while that the hunters were closing in.

Dogs ran up behind her, but she swiped and kicked them away, her loping gait unbroken, and heard the whistle of yet more arrows. These, she was still agile enough to avoid.

With a sharp turn through narrow trees just wide enough for her antlers, she broke away from the chase. The two remaining hounds followed. She dispatched them with another heavy paw.

Then the forest floor opened.

The branches hung lower here, but the snow was flat, bare and level but for a few rocks breaking its perfect surface.

She couldn't afford to stop in doubt.

She leapt out into the expanse, jumping from one carefully chosen stone to another, leaving no mark upon the snow until she reached the trees on the other side.

Here, exhaustion set in.

She wavered and lay down, her body steaming, and licked at the graze on her thigh.

She'd fallen still by the time the hunters discovered her.

"Exhaustion," one of the liveried men declared. "She gave a good chase." He dismounted from his panting horse, the others following suit, and stepped towards the clearing.

"It's a river, milord," another called out, one of the last to step down.

"I can see that," he replied impatiently, "but snow doesn't settle on moving water, Jerose. It's long frozen. We go."

The raghorn's panting breath rose in fine, wispy clouds, her ribs heaving in fatigue. She didn't raise her head.

Not until the first splash and shrieks of shock.

She pushed herself back up to her feet and watched the nine hunters flail in the freezing water, scrambling and failing to haul themselves back out onto the snowdrifts that crumbled beneath their every attempt. The blanket of snow-covered duckweed and water-crowfoot broke up and bobbed around them. A few vanished beneath the surface as they mistook it for support.

Two of the rocks sank and moved slowly out towards them, trailing algae-frond hair.

The raghorn snorted her satisfaction and limped away.

# Step Lightly

*Ferraden*

Tapering black branches interlocked and tangled the strip of midnight sky far above the river. The forest was caged. Birds flew through the flicker of moonlight; black shapes melded into the rest and brought the sky to life before vanishing east and west into the dark.

The sight was blurred by rings across the water, cast by the falling snow. But the disturbance moved no deeper. There was nothing to mask the pounding tremor of clumsy feet, reverberating through the river.

The runner soon flashed into sight above along the bank.

A cloak of green shrouded the figure, no doubt a proud garment once but now tattered and worn, its ivory hem splattered like his pale skin with blood. It was the only colour to be seen in the woods, but even that was bleached out by the distant, rippling moon.

There was a sword upon his hip, glinting beneath the cloak whenever the breeze flipped the fabric's edge, and he ran on heavy, steel feet that clattered valiantly through the night. But the quake from his steps didn't share the same tenacity as those of his brothers in arms.

This lone man, pulling the cloak even tighter about his hunching shoulders, ran with the halting, stumbling steps of someone who had nowhere to go, yet knew only that he had to keep moving. His feet faltered and scuffed as he threw desperate glances back over his shoulder every few heartbeats, looking all around himself as though everything was an enemy, and that the bundle he clutched possessively in his shaking arms was to be protected at any and all cost. There was a desperation in his gait, as though he knew that whatever he was fleeing from was already clawing into his back.

His presence was impossible to lose. Shadow, reflection, tremor, loosened snow kicked up and across the water. He would be easy to track. And he wouldn't wander. Humans liked to follow the rivers. Rivers led to safety. It would take him to a village where he could find food and shelter, find help, find a healer. Water was safety.

Water was life.

His valiant boots slipped again in the ice.

A muffled, bitter curse reverberated as another cloud sprayed across the surface. But he ran on, scrambling over roots, fallen trees, negotiating around the drooping crystal willows, steadying himself against rocks. He never parted more than a few paces from the river for an easier path, as though he thought it might vanish if he turned his back for a moment.

This man wasn't the first of his kind to come this way; a coward, or one perhaps with enough good sense to turn away from bloodshed. And they were always desperate. So desperate that the sheer darkness of the trees, the shifting shadows, the closing, clawing branches of the vakehn's magic didn't deter them from entering the forests.

But they never got far. Lost and confused in the unnatural tangle of the overshadowing woods, they always succumbed to something, no matter which route they took.

He stopped suddenly at the edge of an overhang and stared off into the south-western forest. The underside of those trees flared as though the stars were falling through them, flashing and popping in and out of existence, illuminating the depths of the night and casting the frost into the blues of the morning sky and the lilac of sunset.

Shards of light pierced the water, and a maddened fusion of wailing and cackling tumbled haphazardly through the current.

The steel-booted man spun where he stood, feverish eyes searching frantically through the forest as he pulled his cloak tighter again. But whatever he sought or wondered, he found no answer.

He snapped quickly back towards the river, to his hope, his salvation, and traced it as far as it could be seen. But through the snow-clogged bushes and blanketed rocks that shaded the water from the banks, there was no certainty that it wouldn't lead him straight to the source of the chaos.

Even so, he saw no choice.

He turned and ran, pounding back along his steps until he came to a ford where the riverbed rose. He waded through it without hesitation. Ripples scattered far and wide.

His feet froze in his boots, but he kept moving, stamping one foot quickly after the other, glancing nervously along its length even as he reached the far bank. Once again, he stuck close, running and stumbling alongside the black, guiding flow.

The south-western trees were still alight when he drew level with them again, but the flashes across the undersides of the glinting leaves came faster now, brighter, and the resonant, mournful cackles had grown in lunacy. But this time, he didn't stop. His feet pounded on, fired by some small drop of comfort for the barrier between them, and followed its stream as it veered abruptly in the opposite direction.

He kicked up another cloud in relief, and battled his way across the outcroppings of rock beside it.

He didn't seem to notice that the expected, blinding eruption of fire didn't come from that pocket of trees, nor that the wailing had ceased. The tremor of his boots didn't falter. He didn't dare hesitate for a moment.


The silver light trickling through the caging branches far above faded as the moon drifted away, leaving the ribbon of sky a deep, abyssal black and the treetops drowning within it. The night aged; the air almost crystallised. The remaining light danced, fragmented through the water.

The haggard soldier finally stopped, his breath short and ragged, escaping in rampant puffs. He'd been running for miles, pink-faced through cold and exhaustion, and now stared blindly into the water as he plunged in his empty waterskin. The movement distorted his shape, but the gash across his eye and nose was clear, as well as the blisters on his hands. He'd worn full armour. There were marks of its wear on his skin. He'd shed it for a quick escape.

He reached in again and splashed the icy water across his face, hissing in shock. But it stirred him. His pink eyes were wider and sharper, and searched through the rippling reflection of snow and forest on the surface as though he might glimpse someone sneaking up behind him.

He didn't notice the face staring up at him from beneath.

He turned away with a breath of forced relief, his movements slower, attempting to encourage some kind of peace of mind, and sat against a willow in the snow. His hand slipped into the bundle he'd been clutching and pulled out something to eat.

A shriek shook the water before he could finish the meagre ration.

Terror ripped him sharply to his feet and he searched feverishly through the trees, but no matter how hard his tired eyes scoured, there was nothing within the black tangle of branches.

Even so, he didn't risk lingering. He pulled his cloak tight again, grasped his bundle, and fled. His frozen feet scuffed and caught no less often.

The river rolled on, bowing and straightening, veering and falling, winding and weaving unstoppably. Overhangs grew taller and darker, icicles reached down from the ledges to spear the water, and slip banks grew wider, littered with snow and wild footprints. And where the black flow deepened, the surging currents built them both higher and wider still.

The sky was shifting; the splaying black branches high above were just visible against a sheet of creeping indigo. The soldier had run all night, and the desperate pounding of his feet had depleted to a drag. He stumbled, he slipped, his cloak snagged on powdered bushes, and his clothes had soaked through where he'd leaned against frozen tree trunks to catch his breath.

Finally, he could go no further.

He staggered against another willow and looked about the forest. There was nothing around but trees. Nowhere to shield himself from the rising, condemning daylight, nor from his own desperate, strangling shame.

He leaned heavier against the frosted wood. The shake from his feet was uncertain, but when he made the effort to move forwards, they didn't lift at all.

He slid down the trunk and collapsed into tears.

Defeated, hysterical sobs trickled through the water.

The fun was had; the hunt, the stalk. The prey was broken. It would run no more. It was time to end it.

Its maw opened.

The sweet and aching melody rose from the water like a mist. It was a song that should surely have graced only the fairest ears in the finest halls - a melody tinted with such sadness, such longing, such hope, that it could only have been crafted by the Goddess Herself, and played only upon a violin of the most sacred spruce.

A song that reached into the heart and filled it with exquisite promises.

The soldier rose slowly to his feet. His empty red eyes were fixed to the glittering water, to the fine flakes of snow that fell like diamonds to its surface. All anguish, all desperation had fled his features, and the gradual stride of his frozen feet was finally assured.

He stepped down the bank, his boots clattering valiantly. His sword glinted proudly at his side. His tattered cloak hung loose at his back, picked up by a passing breeze. His bundle lay forgotten in the snow.

His boots broke the water. The chill rushed in between the plates, but he didn't pause or flinch.

The water rose above them, soaking into his clothes. His skin prickled, but he didn't recoil.

His hands brushed the surface, and submerged. He didn't pull them out.

The water passed his waist.

The näck's head broke the surface and watched him with slanted eyes and thin, frog-like pupils. But the soldier didn't run. His calm didn't break. Even as the small, green arms entangled about him and pulled him beneath the river.

There was no struggle.

Bubbles popped quietly at the surface.

He hadn't once wondered why the lazy, frozen water was still flowing.

*Fifty five days.*

*Fire scarred her mottled skin. Cut, burned and abused; blood stained even her bones, her veins split open and dammed by a relentless need for perfection.*

*Her body was broken. Lashed and pinned and trampled, she couldn't fight back. She couldn't defend herself alone. She couldn't beg. She couldn't threaten. She couldn't escape.*

*Strength had slipped away, of body and mind. Her composure was plagued by impossibilities, by things she didn't understand, yet that others used so easily against her.*

*Her vision darkened. There was little light to see but that of the flames that tormented her, and little blue above but the flare of magic.*

*Silently, Turunda screamed.*

# Chapter 17

The valley was white, but dark, the strange light of the snow overpowered by the interlocking canopy. The trunks beneath emerged a deep, stony brown where the frost shrank from the bark, and the earth around them was patchy with thawing soil. The snow here was finally beginning to melt. But it brought Hlífrún little joy to see it.

The leaves had turned black and limp without the frost to support them, and the wildflowers that had been pierced by its tiny crystal blades lay dead and scarred on the ground. There were carcasses dotted along the slopes; dead mice, dead birds, all defeated by the cold and as yet untouched by predators, themselves having moved off to hunt and struggle elsewhere.

So much had suffered. So much had died. And even as she coaxed out the warmth of life, the chill itself remained. The trees only had so much in them to give.

So did she.

Hlífrún leaned against a towering beech tree half way down the forested slope, watching the dark river flow along the valley and the deer and boar that drank from the edges. Fatigue slowed her veins even while frustration and an unshakable anger fired the sap within them. This had all taken so long. The joining of the chasms, the borders completely split - only woven roots connected the mykodendrit to the rest of her domain now. Turunda had been as good as torn away from the rest of the continent.

She was stretched in all directions, exhausted, furious, and couldn't remember the last time she'd either slept or smiled.

A breeze rolled in, peeling yet more thin flakes of bark from her body. She barely noticed.

Her painite eyes flicked further down the river and watched the deer and boar vanish into the forest. The despairing pang of loneliness they left behind them hit her like the wind.

She stubbornly tore herself back out of it, and stepped away from the tree to stand defiantly on her own two feet. She would not succumb to such a useless sentiment. She was doing all she could, and it was working - slowly, but surely - and she would give all she had to see it done. However much or little that was. She was not impotent. She was not helpless. That her mind tried to convince her otherwise only angered her.

As did the Mage. For that wretched oaf had been plaguing her thoughts increasingly often lately. According to him, the Ghost was at fault for the chasms - who only knew why? - but the Mage had *assured* her he would handle it while she kept everything alive. And yet, as far as the evidence showed, his power was proving *useless!* There were no results, the chasms were growing and spreading out of control, moving faster than any others over the rest of the continent! Her world was falling apart around her, and he was taking his *time!*

She bit off a snarl and balled her fists.

*Accursed humans.* To think she'd begun to put her trust in one... She was the fool.

His damnable face appeared in her mind as the surrounding plants shook with her ire. Pale, lined, grumpy. Aged before its time. Handsome, she supposed, in a tormented sort of way. And often a touch alarmed - though she was sure that was something she brought out in him.

She caught the slightest bow of her lips and growled in irritation.

There was some affection for him still.

She leaned back against the tree, absently interlocking the grooves of her rough and chiselled shoulder with that of the bark, and sighed.

Yes. *Fine.* She was being irrational. Not all the humans were trying to kill them - though those that *were* were zealous in their attempts - just as not all of *her* kin were trying to kill *them*. The vittra and vakehn alike were trying to discourage them instead, for the most part. Those who weren't trying to burn, flood or stab them, at least. But there would always be enough antagonistic, selfish or heedless humans to revive every altercation, to maintain every prejudice. The idiocy that stalked civilisation would never stop without something extreme to adjust their perspective.

She doubted that this would be enough. And she wasn't prepared to hold back and let her world die so that they could be pushed to the brink of *theirs* through their own blind dependence.

Her heart sank at the recurring thought. She'd read the lines of

Feira's stars enough. One day, it *would* come to exactly that.

But it wasn't this day.

Her eyes trailed back down to the river as the noisy humans finally arrived. Big and small, on foot, on horse, on wagons, and laden with packs, blankets and rounded shoulders. Even the children.

These were not the first refugees to cut through the valley, running from the war. And she wondered how much more damage *this* group would do as they passed.

She didn't wait to find out.

She slipped into the beech tree and vanished. Both she and the valley were too tired, and the anger and worry over every human presence was as exhausting as her efforts against them.

The leaves shook with delight as Hlífrún emerged into the royal glade, and finally she breathed a little easier. Once splintered and feathered with rime, this revered pocket of forest was now largely free from the snow, and tended frequently to heal the damage the cold had done. The leaves were still sick and limp, and no flowers grew nor coloured the numb air with their scent, but it glowed with hope nonetheless.

And her throne was the most vibrant of all. Shaped from ancient growths and modified roots put forth freely by the venerable yew, it was draped and cushioned with spongy moss that crept over the old, thick trunk, impossibly bright and vivid in the darkness of the grove. Even the encircling fungi and smooth river stones placed at its foot seemed to glow.

But the lift in Hlífrún's mood was fleeting. Here, the weariness seemed to set in that much faster.

She dropped heavily into her throne and settled deep into its familiar comfort, her fingertips already moving absently over the surface of the mossy arm rests, just as they always did. The tip of her cow-tail flicked as it draped over the side.

Her consciousness melted into the old giant and connected to the forest, drawing her deeper than she could have been anywhere else, seeing, feeling and knowing every blade of smothered grass, and all that flourished beyond.

Then she was ripped right back out.

Hlífrún's eyes flashed wide open.

The all-too-familiar sensation of her body and soul each being torn apart staggered the breath from her. She doubled over, thrown from her seat by the convulsion, and hit the thawing earth hard.

Her soul was still within the tree. She could feel the earth shaking deep below, feel it splintering, yawning, snaking from the west.

From far too near.

And coming closer.

Panic flashed white behind her eyes.

"*No!*"

The Queen of the Woods leapt to her feet as fast as she could without stopping to catch her breath, her spirit returning as she melded into the nearest tree. She leapt out again a heartbeat later, just ahead of the rolling destruction. There was no time to wonder at what had triggered it. She could still feel the natural magic of her glade - she was barely outside of it, and the rift was moving much too fast towards it.

She dropped to her knee and plunged one hand down into the soil, commanding its defence, shifting the roots, strengthening their tangles to hold it all together.

But it was no good.

The chasm surged ahead and broke through the encircling trees.

"*My throne will not fall!*" The words ripped like splinters from her throat.

But sacrifices had to be made. And burdens had to be split.

She slammed both her hands down into the earth and plunged her spirit into the roots. Immediately, they stirred into action. Those that lashed out from the rend pierced and anchored into the opposite banks, while those ahead of the destruction moved like snakes through the undergrowth, growing, reaching and twining together, stabilising the soil and holding the earth closed.

More bark peeled away from her skin, and the cracks that splintered from her hollow-bark back grew wider under her strain.

The rend began to slow, but it didn't cease. It moved forwards stubbornly, mindlessly, focused only on growing, growing, growing.

More power was poured into the defence. She ignored the weakness mounting within her, and steeled herself against the drop of the glade's own strength.

Sacrifices had to be made.

Burdens had to be split.

Better to weaken two than lose one entirely.

The glade was filled with the creak and groan of wood, of snapping roots, of buckling efforts, but her mind was closed to all of it and the trees continued their willing fight. Those roots that snapped reached out and tried again; those that buckled were replaced by others. The trees that swayed and creaked and groaned gave every measure of strength they had, until, finally, the rift's advance slowed to a crawl.

Then, at last, to a stop.

Her chest continued to heave and shudder with the hammering of her heart. Her sap boiled. Her jaw was set so hard her teeth were ready to crack.

Her eyes flashed open and flicked around. The glade looked little different - the weave of the roots beneath the grass had changed, but that was all. Every tree still stood, the surface of the rift remained out of sight, and the yew and its throne were untouched.

But she could feel the weakness.

The honoured glade had no strength left to thaw itself.

The furious clench to her jaw didn't loosen as she rose shakily back to her feet, empowered, at least for the moment, by rage and adrenaline.

The vakehn that had come at the suffering plea of the woods remained on their knees, connected to the roots, already doing what they could to replenish the glade's vitality. They were oblivious to the murderous silence their Rötternas Moder left behind her as she stepped wordlessly into the bark of a tree.

It was time she had a word with the Mage.

'His way' was taking far too long.

# A Curiosity Thoroughly Unsatisfied

*Greentop*

The old vittra sat warmly bundled in his tattered wools, his hat pulled low over his head, scarf wrapped high, eyes closed and pleasantly oblivious to the world. The breeze was slack, thank the stars, and the gently drifting snow was thin. He heard a grunt and the tinkle of a bell beside him as the big, white goat shook the flakes from her fur, but didn't stir himself, even as the melt flicked onto his long, numb nose. He sat there in stillness for some time, moving only to puff, fiddle and tamper his pipe.

It wasn't until a presence moved forwards into the quiet afternoon that he finally opened one eye and glanced lazily through the forest from his perch upon the rock. Someone was near. It was a fairly profound presence, in fact - magic, he reckoned, and powerful at that. And there were others of far less consequence following it.

He took another long draw upon his pipe. "Well, well." He looked down towards the goat. "We have a wanderer of esteem today, Etta."

She didn't lift her head from the snow, nor even bother to grunt in disinterest.

The vittra tutted to himself and returned to his disconnected watch of the afternoon, but he soon found himself following the path of the Mage all the same. It was him, without a doubt. He never travelled alone.

He shook his head in pity.

That poor man - he was nothing exceptional, so far as he knew, no different from any other mage but for the fact that he had control over his magic. Not that control was rare. In fact it was others' *loss* of it that was unusual. This fellow should've passed by without notice. But, unfortunately for him, he'd decided to meddle in the magic gathering at ruins, and had succeeded where others had failed in removing some isolated effects. That alone had earned him the misfortune of ensnaring Hlífrún's fascination and being charged with removing *all* the magic throughout her forests. He'd rather wisely agreed to it, though he'd not had much choice, but only under the condition that he be allowed to handle it his own way. The vittra had no idea what that meant, and it seemed the Root Mother herself was equally in the dark.

She seemed to blame him for the snow to some degree, too, even though that was nothing more than the result of other mages' incompetence - humans playing with things they didn't understand with no clue of how to fix their mistakes. That was nothing unusual, either. They probably weren't even trying. Too busy squabbling like children.

He tampered the pipe again, pressing the burning tobacco deeper into the well, and looked around surreptitiously for any watching kvistdjur that might take offence.

All clear.

He continued to puff away quite happily.

Perhaps that was why she held the Mage responsible. She believed he was the only one that could reverse it. She and the vakehn could coax out the warmth of life from the trees until they were sprouting leaves from their own eyeballs, but they would never succeed in eradicating the snow, not fully. It was magic that had caused it, and only magic of a similar strain could take it away, and that meant humans had to do it themselves.

He supposed that was ultimately why the Mage was so important to her. Humans wouldn't listen to her, and her manipulation over their minds with spindle-fingers mushrooms could only go so far, and only for so long. It needed a more direct approach. And since she didn't have the means to obliterate humans completely, that approach had to come from within the humans' own world.

A sudden lash of fright froze his spine. The latest draw of smoke began burning his tongue, but it was a long moment before he was able to release it.

As subtle as the Mage's arrival was, Hlífrún's was impossible to miss. Her presence was like a thunderclap at the best of times. Now it was like lightning flashing and eviscerating the trees and setting everything around it alight.

She was not happy. And there was only one reason she was here.

An itch of curiosity prickled the skin on the back of the vittra's neck. Actually it was more like a clawing rake than an itch. But he was not going to eavesdrop. Not because he wasn't curious, but because Hlífrún would notice, and he didn't much fancy a tangle with her - at least, not in this mood. Her nature had always been temperamental - quick to anger, quick to delight - but now she was set firmly in unremitting rage. Though that, he supposed, at least meant she was predictable.

...Even so...

His narrow eyes dropped thoughtfully to Etta. He'd been sat there for quite a while. The goat could do with a walk. The poor thing was probably out of her mind with restlessness by now.

"Come along, Etta," he muttered, picking up the leash to her bridle and hopping down from the rock, his pipe held with practised grip in his teeth. He tugged at the goat, who bleated irritably as she was torn from her slumber, harried her to her hooves and led her at a forced amble further along the river.

He didn't risk going too far - just enough to spot the pale, dark-haired mage through the trees, and Hlífrún before him, flanked by three kvistdjur and two vakehn. A little excessive, perhaps, but menace was on her mind. But, in that case, her ire alone would've been enough - couple that with the fact that she'd made no attempt to cover herself for the sake of human sensitivity, she'd probably startle them into submission in moments.

He dragged his eyes away from her perfect form and looked instead to the others. The Mage's companions were out of sight - hanging back or maybe rooted in place. But they weren't the Root Mother's concern. Even so, he wondered if any of them were armed. It would be foolish not to be, given the sorry state of the world - but displaying weapons in the forests given the state *they* were in... Thinking about it, there was probably no right answer to that situation.

The vakehn were both armed, but only with bows. At such close range, they were only for show. Aside from Hlífrún herself, the kvistdjur were the most likely threats. Their wooden talons were a thing of nightmares.

The head of one snapped suddenly in his direction.

He drew too quickly on his pipe in shock and spun away on the pretence of tending his goat. He managed not to cough and splutter. And the kvistdjur didn't approach. If it had, it would've already been standing beside him.

He dared to turn back just in time to see Hlífrún lash out towards the Mage, and him stagger back a step. The vittra made a quiet grunt of approval. At least he wasn't as arrogant as other humans. Nor cowardly, he supposed. He stood his ground better than could be expected.

He watched as the Mage began gesticulating, and grumbled quietly to himself. He couldn't really hear much, even despite the quiet afternoon. But he wasn't about to risk getting close enough to try. He'd have to make do.

She was probably only chastising him anyway, blaming him for his kind's faults, questioning his abilities, his loyalty, his competence - degrading him and prolonging the torment to scare out an explanation.

He'd rather like one too, really. Forests aside, the snow wasn't doing his own family any good. If nothing else, there was little for old Etta to graze, and that meant milk was thin - which also meant little cheese, little cream, and little butter. And when they had to feed her their oats instead, that meant less bread and even less porridge. And a vittra needed his porridge.

A raised voice. She'd said something to offend him - he'd missed it, because he'd been thinking about porridge - and the Mage shouted back, daring a step forwards.

She moved closer in answer. She must have given him one of her terribly calm threats, because he jerked back again a hot second later.

He watched them closely for a while, but beyond another brief bout of gesticulation - defensive, it seemed - little else happened.

Etta soon lay down in boredom, and he leaned against her great, shaggy bulk, puffing ceaselessly on his pipe. She bleated as a shift of the wind carried a cloud of smoke across her velvet nose, snaring again the kvistdjur's attention.

He cursed and turned as quick as he had the first time, straddled her back leg and feigned a study her perfectly trimmed hooves. When he found a rock wedged between them, however, he drew a knife from his pocket and busied himself with removing it.

He looked back up only when he noticed that the quarrel had fallen silent, and watched the Mage take another careful step forwards. A hopeful one.

The vittra muttered a curse. What had he missed?

The Root Mother stepped towards him and passed, no doubt,

another deadly quiet remark. Then she spun away, her rich, wild, cascading mane flaring like a fire around her, and stormed off into the trees.

The Mage hurried forwards, his hand reaching out after her, and shouted her name with definite exasperation. This, he heard clearly, and heard it just as he felt her presence vanish.

She was gone. And the kvistdjur had flashed away too.

The Mage's hand dropped in defeat.

The vittra, too, sighed in disappointment, and nudged Etta back to her feet. His curiosity was very far from satisfied.

# Into The Face Of Doom

*Sagestone*

Hlífrún tracked the crooked line of the branch her head rested upon, following it upwards as it split into two, then each of those into three, and higher still along their gnarled, tapering lengths until the thinnest twigs curved and craned up towards the heavy, grey sky.

A numbing breeze jostled the drops of ice-cold water thawing from the leaves. She barely flinched as the tiny pocket of downpour freckled her sprawling body; she continued to stare impassively up through the reaches, watching the dense ceiling of cloud beyond undulate, darkening, lightening then darkening again as it reorganised itself at the wind's direction.

The chill was weak in this wooden bubble. The old chestnut tree had much warmth to breathe, and it gave it willingly. She was grateful. She had little strength left to beg.

Her limbs felt weighted as she lay in the boughs of the stoic giant, her body listless and unresponsive. She was quite certain she'd be unable to move if she tried.

Her eyelids had grown heavy, her mind slow, lost in the hopeless, subduing depths of melancholy. Exhaustion had gripped her soul the tightest of all. And her meeting with the Mage those five days ago had done little but spur it along.

He had a plan, he'd assured her of that, but remained convinced that his 'Ghost' was the root of the problem - of both the chasms *and* the war. And so the Ghost remained his focus. *'Fight the cause, not the symptoms.'* She couldn't argue with that. There was no use picking out an infestation of wight borers one bug at a time if the nest remained untouched and thriving at the centre of the tree trunk. But the longer it took to find a way to remove that nest, the more harm those individual borers would do. And the more irreparable the damage.

But the chill...the biting, breaking, piercing chill... He had little to say on that beyond 'I'm working on it'.

Hopelessness burrowed its way deeper into her heart. The chill wasn't going anywhere any time soon. The safety of the wilds remained squarely upon her shoulders. Just as it always did.

Her breath moved with the breeze, drawn out in a dejected sigh. She gave in at last to the weight of her eyelids.

Sixty days. The moon had changed twice since this had started. It could change twice more before it was done. Maybe five times more. Maybe seven.

She doubted it would be tomorrow.

And all she could do in the mean time was continue as she had been, making an ant's stubborn progress up a mountain while trying to ignore any possibility of failure.

Another icy shower from the wilted leaves encouraged her to finally gather the will to rise.

Strips of bark peeled away from her as she dropped from the branches, but she landed quietly, steady and graceful on her feet, and set off without another wasted moment. There was more she needed in this forest than unity with the trees.

And it didn't take long to find it.

Her heart sank further as the forest thinned up ahead, and her efforts to steel it were fruitless. She knew what she would find. She knew how it would feel, knew how it would look, and knew how it would haunt her. But she kept walking anyway.

At least here, the numbing absence of scent on the air was a blessing.

Her heart hammered as the tree line loomed ahead, and all but burst as the forest suddenly fell away around her. But she continued to put one grey foot in front of the other as she stepped out into the blinding white of the overcast sky, brighter still above the dark, mud-churned snow, and her eyes traced over the scene with forced detachment.

Long, thin shafts like branchless trees stood slanted in the broad, unnatural clearing, black against the forward sky. The pennants at their tips hung lifeless in the muted air.

Lines of wood, of stakes and logs, stood shattered across the tree-felled field, some still gasping a fine plume of black smoke, and others further out, dumped or fallen, stared with flashes of more misplaced colour.

Slivers of light glinted quietly here and there, shields and swords dropped or stabbed into the slushed ground, and others of armour, inexplicably removed and cast aside, or encasing still the pale, glass-eyed soldiers.

A meek breeze stirred the tattered pennants, but they moved limp. Whatever pride they'd snapped in before had left them as the life had left their bearers.

She kept walking through the carnage, through the snow trampled and dyed with blood. She didn't spare a glance at the jet-black crows that cawed and hopped and picked over the dead, nor for the foxes and wolves that roamed at the edges. She saw only what was absent.

There had been a forest here when the snow had come. Now it was lost, cut down for war machines, then burned, and then twisted into a battleground. A hunting ground, once; a home, a mating arena. Now it was a graveyard.

And yet, even as she walked on light and sombre feet, she found herself waiting. Waiting for the tears. Waiting for the rage. Waiting for her tail to twitch. Waiting for the site and all its injury to hit her with the force she'd expected of it.

But instead, her head spun. Her perspective felt almost tilted, and her eyes were not her own.

She held no hope that the stupor would last. Because this wasn't all.

It was never all.

She neared the far side of the battlefield. It had been kind so far. But as she approached the furthest trees, she felt her numbed heart begin to race once again.

She stopped beside a blackened tree and placed her hand upon its peeled, skeletal trunk. Her lips pulled downwards, and her eyes dropped slowly to the corpse at its foot, half-buried in the snow. Askafroa were not as plentiful as they'd once been, but even back then, every loss had been a keen one, for their ash tree always followed. This one had been caught in the clearing fire. An unintended victim - which only made her fall more tragic.

She moved on without a word. She didn't dare part her lips to even whisper the apology that gathered behind her teeth.

She came then upon several blackened kvistdjur, each as smothered as the ash-wife. They would have seemed to any wanderer as fallen trees and branches half-protruding from the snow. Perhaps even ideal kindling. She couldn't know. She didn't burn her trees. Nor could she make such a blind mistake. She knew only too well what they were, and what pain they'd felt when they'd died.

Her jaw hardened. Her lips pulled lower. She tore her eyes away.

They landed only moments later on yet more torment. Four dead Arkhamas, and untouched by the snow. Their injuries were frozen, but plain. They'd fallen after the burning, cut down by steel.

But by whose hand?

The Arkhamas appeared as human children but for their ashen skin and giant, mischievous eyes. While the ghosts, the worst of human kind, could butcher them so easily without a thought at all, the wounds weren't nearly neat enough for that. Could the soldiers really have done it? Men with families and young of their own?

If they were misled then startled by their eyes, perhaps. In groups, human stupidity flourished.

Her jaw clamped harder. Her teeth threatened to break. Her twisted lips pursed. But the tears still sprung into her eyes. The impetuous little fools. So zealous, so determined...

Another glint drew her blurred gaze beyond them, then another, and another still as the tears welled and caught up the light. Her lips broke into a proud smile. These four wore none of the marks of a warband, and yet they'd taken out eleven soldiers storming through their home before falling themselves. And if they'd had help, it was from others of their kind. There were none of the tell-tale wounds of harpy strikes.

Her eyes moved back to the forest children as her anguish finally rolled down her cheeks. But her anger was quickly smothered by fatigue. Her kind were perishing in a battle they had no use of. They were not part of the humans' war, and they had done nothing to incite an assault on themselves. And yet...all this...

All this.

She rose back to her feet.

She was exhausted, but she had no options. Giving up was unacceptable. Even at her most listless, she had never entertained it as a choice. Without her, the wilds *would* fall. And she could not fail Feira. Not after all these millennia. Not to magic, nor to steel.

She moved on through the forest, not daring to flee back to her grove, not allowing herself the indulgence of looking away. She walked, she looked, and she steeled. However long this lasted - two moons, five or seven - she would fight it to the end.

Because, most importantly, she could not fail the creatures that had already given their lives to answer her call to arms.

*Seventy one days.*

*Foreboding laced the air like a poison. There was no shriek or song of bird, there was no buzz or chirp of insect. Even the breeze itself had choked. There was only the faintest hum, an incorporeal tremor, as though something ponderous yet powerful was rumbling awake.*

*Rabbit and raghorn froze and strained against the deafening silence. Eagle and dragonfly observed like stone from their perches. Vittra gathered and muttered apprehensions, kvistdjur stared through the shadows, Arkhamas climbed higher and peered through the branches, näcken watched from beneath crystalline water.*

*Gradually, a rippling smudge began to fog the horizon. Every eye watched it, fixated with stifled breath as it grew gradually hazier, gradually thicker, until it shifted from a vapid contortion to a tangible cloud, yet void of mist or substance. They watched as it rolled, engulfing more and more of the forests with every passing second, all while heading inexorably closer, leaving a world of darkness in its wake.*

*A distinct and familiar horror swept out ahead of it.*

*Instinct scattered them in a heartbeat, flying, burrowing, running and diving, even as their bones promised them it couldn't be escaped.*

*Hlífrún had the terrible sense that she'd felt all this before.*

# Chapter 20

The rumble intensified.

Like the groan of a distant avalanche, it moved through the bones of the ancient land, reverberating through its veins, through its shrouded skin, and up into the trees to shake their frozen branches as though Turunda herself quaked in terror.

The Queen of the Woods snapped away from the crystallised wych-elm, her fierce eyes firing westward and searching out for miles through the silvered trees. The sensation that roared through her bones and ripped her breath away was no less paralysing the second time.

The vakehn sensed it, too. Both rose swiftly from their tasks to sweep sharp and cautious eyes through the densely wooded scowles, haunted by a memory still fresh enough to sting. Their breath tightened, their shoulders knotted, readied for whatever action was needed to uphold their promise to the wilds. Neither dared entertain the screaming notion that there was nothing that could be done.

Their queen's low, ferocious growl narrowed their search.

Their hearts shuddered before they steeled.

A distortion rippled through the trees, a low, visible, eddying wind that whipped across the bone-white ground, leaping out in all directions like the panicked scatter of deer. But for all its chaos, it surged intently forwards, ever closer, ever nearer, and dragged something unnatural along with it that left a darkness to the forest in its wake.

There was no time for orders. In a heartbeat the vakehn dropped to their knees and thrust their palms against the ground, their fingers reaching out to find contact with the interlocking roots of as many trees and plants as possible, extending their own wild magic, their own will, their own protection to as much of the forest as they could.

But Hlífrún didn't move.

While the two forest wardens set diligently to work, she merely stood and stared, watching the rapid, swelling, imminent wind with wide and incredulous eyes.

It crashed down upon them in moments.

She didn't stagger. Even as it pulled at her dark mane, tangled around her twiggy crown and peeled yet more paper-thin bark from her body, she didn't move. Only one thought hung in her mind, and it remained there even as the wind rolled on and away behind her.

Shock squeezed a sharp, absent breath from her chest.

Then the darkness slipped in, moving around them like a creeping tide.


Slowly, the vakehn rose to their feet. Their wary, apple-green eyes surveyed the engulfing shadow. It had seeped into everything, every fold, every crevice, and smothered even the chill from the air.

The strange, self-emitting light of the snow had dimmed. The brightness of the silver trees had dulled. Even the glint of the crystal leaves had shattered all around them.

The mistrustful furrow of their brows deepened even as the prickle of their dark skin smoothed in the summer warmth.

"...He's done it..."

Their eyes turned slowly upon Hlífrún.

The skogsrå queen still stared motionless through the old forest, her voice slipping out in an absent whisper, her painite eyes wide as she watched the natural darkness deepen around her.

Her eyes flicked suddenly towards the leaves of the old wych-elm, bright with a foolish hope. But the foliage of it - of *every* tree - was the same beneath the thaw: black, wilted, and frost-bitten.

Her regal face transformed at the hole that split opened in the pit of her stomach. Heartache twisted her lips, disgust wrinkled her nose, and furious tears sprung to finally chase the foolish amazement from her eyes. *'Too sudden...the change...it was too sudden...'*

As fast as the frost had arrived, it had vanished. Just as abrupt, just as jarring, just as violent. The forests would suffer for this. It was yet more unnatural harm to heal, to tend, to reverse - and it could yet happen all over again! Maybe even before the forests had recovered! Now that the humans had done it once, there was nothing to stop them from spreading this biting taint again, intentionally or not - for as long as they meddled, as long as they utilised powers and manipulated elements they didn't understand, the world would never be safe. It would take more than the actions of one to change that.

A vakah stepped into her seething sight, walking slowly on silent feet, looking around in disbelief while the other touched the damp grooves of bark and pushed her heel down into the rapidly appearing soil to see the dark impression left behind.

The purse of her lips tightened as she pulled back her tears. Evidently the truth of the matter hadn't hit them yet.

Her blurred gaze turned vehemently back out to the tormented forest, passing fleetingly over vakehn bow and quiver and enchanted wooden blades as she took in the scale of the destruction.

And slowly, very slowly, an obvious and welcome thought elbowed its way to the front of her mind.

Her brow furrowed deeply.

It could all come again...*but*...this time, she and her kin had fought it. They had fought it, and *survived*. And, by their efforts, the *forests* had survived. They would all do so again. Maybe not her, and maybe not the creatures as she knew them - humans would, no doubt, change the world irreparably first - but nature itself *would* fight back. Again. And again. And again. And civilisation would either learn, or fall.

She straightened defiantly, though the hole in her gut remained half-open, and breathed deeply the scent of creeping damp.

*'But, for today...'*

Her eyes tracked back through the forest as a gentle pattering sound moved towards them from the depths.

"Rain?" One of the vakehn asked. Hlífrún shook her head. Thawing ice; water dropping beneath the trees...but it didn't sound right.

Nothing *would* be right. Not for a long while. But she would help it get there.

She looked once more to the twisted wych and its blackened leaves. "Ignore it." Her voice was as hard as rock. "We have much to do."

"What of his request for aid?"

She didn't turn towards the vakah.

"If what the Mage says about the war and the rifts is true..."

But the queen's attention remained upon the dead leaves.

Without a word of acknowledgement, she reached a wooden hand into the lowest bough and brushed her finger along the wilted, drooping foliage. She forced her incensed heart to slow, coaxed her breath to calm, then slipped into her magic, into the soul of the forest, and murmured with its heartbeat.

With that caress, the whole cluster dropped as easily from the twig as though she'd plucked them. And then, in their place, seven fresh, green leaves began to sprout and unfurl.

Meltwater struck them from the branch above.

Now, the patter sounded right.

Her shoulders relaxed, though she didn't dare let a smile touch her lips. Then she stepped forwards, and melded without a glance into the tree.

"He will have it," her voice dropped like a stone as she vanished. "We take our vengeance upon the Ghost."

And the Ghost would be crushed.

Nature always prevailed.

It had to, or there would be nothing left.

For anyone.

Thank you so much for reading *Hlífrún*, you have no idea what it means to me! Reading is a huge investment of time, and I dearly hope this book was worth your while.

Hlífrún is a stand-alone supplement
to The Devoted trilogy.

Events occur between book two, *The Sah'niir,* and book three, *Veysuul*. The trilogy begins with *The Zi'veyn*.

You can also find me on Patreon, with early access to monthly short stories before they're posted on my website, as well as exclusive snippets of whatever I'm currently working on, access to my random research, illustrations, and be on the top of my list for opportunities, like beta-reading future work, or obtaining exclusive editions.

@KimWedlock
www.KimWedlock.com
www.Patreon.com/KimWedlock

Printed in Poland
by Amazon Fulfillment
Poland Sp. z o.o., Wrocław

62213593R00085